THE L🌰VE BEAN

SIOBHÁN PARKINSON

THE O'BRIEN PRESS
DUBLIN

First published 2002 by The O'Brien Press Ltd,
20 Victoria Road, Dublin 6, Ireland.
Tel: +353 1 4923333; Fax: +353 1 4922777
E-mail: books@obrien.ie
Website: www.obrien.ie

ISBN 0-86278-772-6

British Library Cataloguing-in-Publication Data
Parkinson, Siobhán
The love bean
1.Twins - Fiction 2.Ethnic relations - Fiction 3.Love stories
4.Young adult fiction
I.Title
823.9'14[J]

1 2 3 4 5 6 7
02 03 04 05 06 07

The O'Brien Press receives
assistance from

Editing, typesetting, layout and design: The O'Brien Press Ltd
Printing: Cox & Wyman Ltd

THE LOVE BEAN

PRAISE FOR SIOBHÁN PARKINSON

The Love Bean
'The writing is hugely evocative, the dialogue spot-on, the issues
immensely thought-provoking ... For sheer beauty, and wit, this book
will invite reading many times over'
Inis, the Children's Books in Ireland magazine

Sisters ... No Way!
'Cindy is a tremendously exuberant character. Parkinson has the subtlety,
imagination and skill to create ... wonderfully rounded individuals.
An intelligent, witty and well-written novel'
Books Ireland

Four Kids, Three Cats, Two Cows, One Witch (maybe)
'Not only one of the best Irish children's books of the year,
but I honestly think one of the best Irish children's books
we've ever had, full stop ... It's an amazingly clever book'
Robert Dunbar, 'The Gay Byrne Show'

Call of the Whales
'An adventure with attitude'
The Irish Times

'A captivating coming-of-age tale with a
distinctive narrative voice'
The Irish Independent

Siobhán Parkinson is one of the most highly acclaimed children's writers in Ireland. She has won numerous awards and her books have been translated into several languages, including French, German, Italian, Portuguese, Spanish and Danish. She lives in Dublin with her husband Roger, a woodturner, and their son Matthew, Siobhán's personal literary critic.

OTHER BOOKS BY SIOBHÁN PARKINSON
Amelia
No Peace for Amelia
The Leprechaun Who Wished He Wasn't
Four Kids, Three Cats, Two Cows, One Witch (maybe)
Sisters ... No Way!
The Moon King
Breaking the Wishbone
Call of the Whales
Cows are Vegetarians
Animals Don't Have Ghosts

Dedication

To Kathleen Milne, with thanks for the love bean.

Acknowledgements

Grateful thanks to The Irish Writers' Centre and Dublin Corporation Arts Office and to the Church of Ireland College of Education, Rathmines, Dublin, where I held residencies during the early stages of writing this novel. Both residencies were part-funded by An Chomhairle Ealaíon/The Arts Council.

And what obscur'd in this fair volume lies
    Find written in the margent of his eyes.
This precious book of love, this unbound lover,
To beautify him only lacks a cover.
The fish lives in the sea, and 'tis much pride
For fair without the fair within to hide.
That book in many's eyes doth share the glory,
That in gold clasps locks in the golden story

Romeo & Juliet Act 1, Sc iii

CHAPTER 1

Love is ... a madness most discreet
Romeo & Juliet Act 1, Sc i

Lydia's key scraped in the keyhole. Damn! She'd hoped to sneak in quietly, without anyone noticing. She didn't want any awkward questions before she'd got her story straight in her head. She held her breath for a moment, pressed her ear to the door, and then turned the key another half-turn. In its secret place of cogs and pistons, embedded in the wood of the door, she could feel the lock click open. Still Lydia stood there, her arm extended, the key tensed between her fingers, and listened for sounds on the other side of the door. Nothing.

Gratefully, gently, she pushed the door and slipped around it, into the hall. No one called out. No one appeared. Good. She pressed the door closed again behind her and leaned her back against it. Made it.

A giggle rose up in her. She was behaving like a ridiculous character in a detective movie, sneaking into her own house. It was four o'clock in the afternoon, for goodness' sake. It wasn't as though she'd been drinking cider in the park or smoking behind the bicycle sheds. She'd only been to the second-hand CD shop to sell off a bunch of her least favourite CDs and buy a new one with the proceeds. She'd only met Jonathan Walker there and spent five (fabulous) minutes chatting to him. She'd only agreed to go for a coffee with him tomorrow afternoon in the glitzy seafront cappuccino bar, where the stainless steel equipment gleamed like precious metals and the customers shone like superstars – or so it seemed to Lydia, who didn't shine at all.

There was nothing wrong with meeting Jonathan by chance in a music shop. Nothing wrong, either, she told herself, with agreeing to meet him again. He was stunningly good-looking: high cheekbones, lightly tanned skin, a flop of rich wavy hair over his forehead, widely spaced blue eyes – it was all too good to be true. Lydia had said it herself, six months ago. Anyone who looked like that couldn't possibly be good. Beauty like that was bound to corrupt. Still, no one would have had anything against him, or against Lydia's going to meet him, if it hadn't been for Julia.

But there *was* Julia. There was no getting around that. It was definitely a problem, no matter what way Lydia looked at it.

Julia was Lydia's identical twin. They had the same pale, freckly skin, the same crinkly, red-gold hair, the same grey-green eyes. But that's where the resemblance stopped. With her unruly mane of hair, Julia managed to look as if she didn't own a hairbrush; Lydia wore her hair pinned back with a hair slide or plaited or swinging in a ponytail. Julia wore spangly bracelets and fluorescent boots and tights with Santa Clauses on them, even in the summer, and mad purply embroidered things that swooshed as she walked and got tangled up in machinery; Lydia preferred jeans with runners and T-shirts most of the time, or else just black trousers and what Julia called 'sweet little tops'. Julia spent hours on the phone organising her social life; Lydia had friends, but she didn't much like using the phone.

Officially, Julia was still 'getting over' Jonathan. She'd had an amazing though short-lived reign last term as Jonathan's girlfriend, wandering proudly, slowly, home from school with him, sitting over endless lattes in the cappuccino bar with him. But then somebody else, somebody cleverer, prettier, wittier, blonder and with a neater bum and a navel-revealing dress style and who didn't have a problem ordering 'law-tay' the way they pronounced it on American TV – Julia could never bring herself to do that – had stolen him from right under her nose, and Julia had been in mourning ever since. Nobody was allowed to mention him. He was like a shadow person attached to Julia, always there, always ignored.

Mind you, Julia might be expected to have got over Jonathan by now. The break-up had been three months ago. But getting over Jonathan seemed to suit Julia. It gave her an excuse to slouch around the house, changing TV channels with her big toe from the sofa – the remote was always missing – and complaining about life's unfairness. It was the excuse she used also for sitting in the twins' shared attic bedroom for hours each day, playing endless music by dead rock musicians too loudly. They had to be dead, Julia explained, because that was in keeping with her feelings. At first, Lydia had thought this a little weird but kind of poetic; now she just thought it was self-indulgent – she was starting to get tired of passionate wailings.

It was time to stop feeling sorry for Julia.

You'll never guess who I just met? she rehearsed to herself as she strode down the hall towards the kitchen, from where she could hear her twin's voice complaining to their mother about something. *Jonathan Walker! In the CD shop, imagine!* As soon as she thought his name, Lydia felt a blush racing up her pale, freckle-sprinkled face. *Jonathan Walker*, she thought resolutely to herself again, and again came the rush of blood to her cheeks. *Jonathan Walker*, she persisted, and it seemed to her that perhaps the crimson tide subsided. *That old boyfriend of yours, Julia*, she went on grimly, *Jonathan Walker. God, I thought he must have emigrated, it's been so long.* Her heart was beating too fast, but her cheeks felt reasonably cool now. She might be able to carry it off.

Their mother was ironing. She never did in term time but in the summer she ironed and ironed, as if to make up for term-time domestic neglect. Her daughters always laughed at this summertime ironing frenzy of their mother's, but they loved the hot, clean smell of it and didn't object too strenuously to the piles of freshly smoothed clothes that arrived daily in their bedroom.

'You need a project, Julia,' their mother was saying from the ironing board as Lydia opened the door.

'That's such a schooly word,' moaned Julia, waggling her arm to make her new silver bracelet slide down towards her elbow. 'Can't you stop being a teacher for a minute, Frankie, and just be my mum?'

'Don't call me Frankie,' said their mother, stomping the iron with excessive vehemence up and down the sleeve of one of her daughters' shirts so that she was ironing in as many creases as she was ironing out.

'Hello!' said Lydia brightly.

'Hello, love,' said Frankie.

'Where've *you* been?' asked Julia. Her tone was peevish. 'You're fiddling with your plait. Always a sign you're nervous about something.'

Lydia guiltily dropped the hand that had been playing with her plait and waved the CD she had in her hand.

'Out to get this,' she said. Her voice was high, excitable. She coughed, to try to bring it down a tone. 'You'll never guess who I met?'

'Who?' asked Julia, without much interest, still watching the way the bracelet slithered up and down her arm.

Lydia's resolution failed her. 'Eh – Marni Dolan,' she said, blushing, though she had in fact caught sight of Marni in the distance, so it wasn't a lie, not really. 'Imagine! I thought they'd moved.'

'What made you think that?' asked Julia. 'You're all red. Were you running?'

'Yeah,' mumbled Lydia and then rushed to change the subject. 'I could murder a cup of tea. Anyone?'

'You never drink tea,' said Julia.

'I'm thirsty,' Lydia muttered, pushing her plait over her shoulder while she ran water into the kettle. 'It's hot.'

Julia lost interest.

'I've needed a "project", as you call it, for *months*,' she said, turning back to her mother, 'but you've only just *noticed*. That's parents all over for you, isn't it Lydia?'

'Eh?' said Lydia, plugging in the kettle.

'You can't get their noses out of your business most of the time, constantly ringing you up on your mobile, telling you to come right home, right now, but as soon as you hit a little blip in life, they suddenly develop an urgent interest in painting the spare bedroom, or applying for a new job, and they completely lose interest in you and your problems.'

'Painting the spare bedroom?' said their mother, wonderingly. 'We haven't painted the spare bedroom for years. Though now you come to mention it ...'

'Oh, *Mum*!' said Julia.

'Joke!' Frankie threw her hands up. 'Look, no weapons. I hope you've counted me in the tea, Lydia.'

'Not for me,' said Julia. 'I'm going to see if there's anything on the telly.'

'It's a sin,' said Frankie, as Julia stood up to go, 'a *mortal* sin, to be watching TV on an afternoon like this, when you could be out in the garden.'

'What would I *do* in the garden?' Julia asked from the doorway. 'Sit around pretending to be a garden gnome?'

Frankie ignored her. 'Although I suppose I'd make an exception for Wimbledon,' she called encouragingly to Julia's back.

Julia slammed the door. She hated tennis.

CHAPTER 2

That vast shore, wash'd with the farthest sea
Romeo & Juliet Act 2, Sc ii

For several weeks, it had hurt. A lot. To console herself, Julia'd dreamt about him – awake and asleep – dreamt about Jonathan coming back to her, telling her it had all been a dreadful mistake, that he didn't after all love the Belly Dancer (Julia's name for the navel-flaunting slapper who'd nabbed him), begging her to have him back. In the dreams, she'd opened forgiving arms to him and gone floating off with him into the sunset, violins singing joyously, a single, wavering star piercing the dusky sky.

In reality, she hoped she wouldn't be such a doormat, even in the unlikely event that one half of the dream came true and he did come crawling back to her, all regrets and ready to make amends. She hoped she'd have the strength to turn him away. But that's the advantage of dreams: you don't need to be strong in dreams; in dreams you can be shameless about your desires; when you reach for the stars in dreams, you can find yourself with a fistful of sparkle.

But by now, even the dreams had started to fade. The time was coming when she was going to have to admit that she was 'over' Jonathan. And she *was* over him, she knew it, because she'd started to feel bored as well as lethargic, to wish that something – anything – would happen.

Today she was crouched, as usual, on the window seat in the attic bedroom, her music blaring, also as usual, her knees in their floral leggings hunched under her chin, staring out to sea. The twins' room had a view right over the tops of the neighbours' garden trees, over the high wires of the electric railway, over the squat Martello tower clinging like a fat sea anemone to the coastline, right out to the blue horizon, where the sea shimmered into the sky and the sky dipped into the sea.

She didn't hear the bedroom door opening.

'JULIA!' Lydia yelled over the noise.

Julia started. She jabbed the remote control, which she held between her brightly coloured knees, and a silence you could almost hear filled the room.

'I've brought you a storybook,' Lydia said, holding out her peace offering.

Julia had no idea it *was* a peace offering. She didn't know there was anything to make peace about. She knew nothing about the chance meeting between Lydia and Jonathan yesterday in the CD shop, and the plan to meet again today, this time for coffee.

'A *story*book!' she said. 'We're not *seven*, Lydia.'

They always called novels 'storybooks'. It was one of their little jokes, a reference to their shared childhood. There was no need for Julia to react like that. Still, Lydia smiled determinedly.

'It's all right,' she said. 'It's not a *Harry Potter*.'

Julia had been notoriously unable to read any of the *Potter* books, not when she was younger, not now either. 'Too many *words*,' she'd muttered when asked why.

'It's a twinny book,' said Lydia.

'Oh!' said Julia. A sudden smile chased the irritation from her face. The twins had for years had a shared passion for stories with twins in them. 'Remember the O'Sullivan twins?' she said, her grin broadening.

'*Bockety*!' said Lydia, her voice high and strangulated by a wave of laughter.

Julia and Lydia had gone through a phase, when they were about eight, of trying to *be* those horribly well-brought-up, bright-cheeked English girls with bobs and fringes and an innate sense of fairness. They'd acted out bits from the books, jumping on overflowing suitcases to make them close and cooking sausages over an oil-stove – the sausages had stayed resolutely pink and tasted of paraffin, which just goes to show, Julia had said, that things in books are not like things in life. They were enchanted by the idea of lacrosse, and they'd tied tennis racquets onto a long bamboo-handled feather duster and onto a broom handle so they could have makeshift lacrosse sticks. The racquets and the broom handle had survived the game, but the long-handled feather duster was never the same again.

'It's gone all bockety,' their mother used to complain. 'I can't understand it, I've had it for years, and suddenly it's bockety.'

Ever afterwards the mere mention of the word *bockety* had sent the girls into gales of laughter.

'You don't think we should have grown out of twinny books by now, do you?' asked Julia, sobering up and turning the book over. It didn't look as promising as *Jacob Have I Loved* or *The Story of the Treasure Seekers*, but at least it was by an author she liked.

'I don't see why,' said Lydia. 'You don't grow out of being a twin, after all.' You certainly don't, she thought. She stood up. 'Anyway, I'm off. I have to meet someone,' she added tentatively, half hoping that Julia might ask who, and she'd be forced to confess to Jonathan. This secrecy she'd imposed on herself was weighing her down.

But Julia had gone dreamy again, and Lydia didn't know how to bring her back to the subject. She hesitated for a moment, and then opened the door.

Julia wiggled a finger at Lydia absent-mindedly and turned to look out to sea again. The book had slithered into her lap.

When Julia was younger, she'd imagined that this attic bedroom with its view beyond the tame area of water between the outstretched arms of Howth and Dalkey, right out, out to sea, almost to Wales, gave her an advantage in adventure. *Anything* might come scooting over that stretch of water, and Julia'd be the first to know about it. Not Lydia. Lydia barely glanced out of the window, and then it was just to check the weather in the mornings. But Julia loved this view out over the sea, and she returned again and again to this place, where she'd sat so often through her childhood, for comfort and sustenance, and to dream.

The car-ferry was just coming into view over the horizon. It was only a speck, but Julia knew that shortly the little speck would grow to the size of a bluebottle, and then a mouse and then a cat and then an elephant and finally it would be a ship. It was like the old woman who swallowed the fly – I bet she'll die.

'Well, I'm off,' said Lydia again, holding the door open. 'One of the twins, by the way – in the book I mean – she reminds me of you. But her twin's nothing like me. Still, it's interesting to see what it must have been like to be a twin way back then.'

The door had closed behind Lydia before Julia got a chance to ask what she meant. She sighed and picked the book out of her lap. Lydia was probably only trying to tempt her to read it, saying that one twin was like her. Lydia was always trying to get her to read things. Sometimes she was worse than a teacher. Still, it might be interesting. *The Curiosity Tree* it was called. Julia bent the spine back with a satisfying crack and flicked through the fly-leaves to the beginning of the story.

The Curiosity Tree ❶

Sun´va twitched with impatience and slapped away a fly. In this squinting light, she could not make out, from where she crouched uncomfortably in the highest bough of the curiosity tree, even the dimmest outline of the coast of Caledonia. On cooler days, when rain threatened, the distant coast etched itself with astonishing clarity on the horizon, but today, the intensity of the sea-blue, sky-blue glare shimmered the Caledonian coast out of vision.

When Sun´va was younger, Picts had come dashing over the water from Caledonia on raids, yelling and roaring in the rough Pictish dialect that the Irish couldn't understand, causing war and mayhem among the shore-side colony where Sun´va lived. There was a truce now between her people and the Picts and there hadn't been a raid for years. Still, Sun´va felt it was important to keep a lookout from time to time, just in case.

The curiosity tree was an oak that grew at the edge of the forest, a little apart from the other trees, like a sentinel at the gate into the woods. Standing here where the forest petered out, the gradient of the land steepened and the earth gave way to rock, the tree grew precariously, just holding on with rooty toes to the sloping ground that rose away from the sea. Sun´va's father, Ultan, had named it her curiosity tree because, according to him, she climbed it simply out of curiosity.

Curiosity was fine when she was younger, but now

Ultan said she'd got too old for climbing trees, that it was a childish thing to be doing. He wanted her to start preparing herself for marriage. 'Your mother had her first child already at your age, Sun´va,' he would say, as if she cared about that.

Not a thing had stirred for hours in this high blue summer weather. Sun´va was about to climb down from her perch and wander off home. But just as she was preparing to swing out of her branch, something caught her eye, something out there in the glittering blue. Something that was still well out to sea. She crinkled her eyes against the blaze of the sun and watched for a little longer.

The speck on the horizon gradually swelled and grew and took on shape. She could swear that those were masts, reaching spikily into the sky. Her heart lifted with excitement and immediately sank with fear. Those were not masts to hold the little handkerchiefs of sails the local fishing fleet put up to catch the wind, or the sails of Pictish war boats; they were high, intricate masts, designed to carry enormous, complex sheets. The sails weren't in evidence on this still and sunny day with the sea at its laziest, but the boat seemed to be making good headway over the water all the same. It must have oars as well, Sun´va concluded, but how many oarsmen would you need on a boat that size? Even from this distance, she judged that it must be far bigger than any boat she had ever seen.

Rumours had reached Ireland of a powerful people who came from the lands beyond Britain, a people, it was said, whose terrifying tentacles had stretched far, far beyond their own country. Sun´va wasn't sure she believed the stories about these Romans, as they were called, but now, here, before her eyes, was a mighty ship such as they said the Romans had. And now, look, there was another ship pulling alongside the first, and that speck in the distance was probably a third. What if there were a whole fleet of them, swarming with soldiers! They would surely pillage the crops and steal the beasts, and maybe even capture the youngest and strongest of Sun´va's people as slaves. She must raise the alarm, and quickly. That they should come today of all days, when for once her father had left the settlement undefended!

Sun´va's body had stiffened as she lay on the bough of the tree, and she could feel a knobble on the bark pressing uncomfortably against her ribcage, but she daren't leave until she'd established how many ships there were. She needed to know how great the threat was.

At last the speck grew into a third ship, and no fourth ship had appeared. Three, so. Hardly a fleet. Perhaps it wasn't a real invasion. Maybe they were only on a voyage of discovery. Perhaps they just wanted to trade with the Irish.

But whatever they wanted, Sun´va must move quickly to warn her people. The boats were still well off shore. It was likely she was the only one who knew they were approaching. It was up to her to raise the alarm.

But with Ultan from home, whom should she alert? Rian, her father's steward? He'd have to do. All the younger men, the warriors, had gone with Ultan on his journey south to buy cattle, and only the slaves and farmworkers had stayed behind. She'd have to find Rian. Quick, quick!

She bent one stiffened leg at the knee, and felt the rush of pins-and-needles. There was no time to wait for the prickling to subside, though. As Sun´va swung out of the tree, her foot gave way under her, and she folded onto the ground. Impatiently, she yanked her foot from under her body and chafed it briefly to get the circulation going. Gritting her teeth, she stood up and tested the foot. It was still pricklish, but it held her weight. Right! Away!

Sun´va flew through the forest to the edge of the small, brackish lake where her family's crannog stood. She skimmed over the hidden stepping stones to the crannog in the lake, and burst into the little wattle dwelling house, alarm mounting inside her. No one was there except Gobnat, the aging house-slave. Sun´va called Eva's name, though she knew her sister wasn't there. She must have gone out to the fields or to one of the neighbouring houses to help the women with their spinning and dyeing, weaving and sewing.

'Eva!' called Sun´va again, panic making her voice squeak, but no reply came in the still, suffocating air. She picked up a large wooden ladle and dipped it quickly into the water barrel by the door-opening. She drank gratefully and then ran again, out of the house, over the stepping stones, back to the land, and out into the fields. She ran at random, calling, calling. 'Rian, quick, Romans!'

But there was no sign of Rian either, no sign of another human being, anywhere she looked. There were only the cattle grazing on the pasturelands and the hay ripening in the meadows and the hot yellow sun burning the blue out of the sky.

What was the use? Rian was getting on, and anyway, you couldn't go down to the beach to meet a Roman invasion – could you? – led by a farmhand, however trusted and high-ranking. Ultan could rally a whole army of warriors from among his clients and kinsmen within a day or two, but the only men who lived close enough to muster in a matter of hours were peasants and slaves who had no training in warfare.

Oh well, thought Sun´va, falling to her knees with exhaustion from running in the heat, since there is no one to defend us, let the Romans come, then, and do what they will! Perhaps they will be friendly after all. Perhaps it is only a trade mission. Perhaps they will bring barrels of wonderful foreign liquors and sacks of salt and exotic fruits and spices and fine-woven cloths. Oh yes, we shall have a banquet and welcome these brave sailors and Ultan will toast their health in mead and we shall have music and merrymaking and feasting till dawn and we will have a pig slaughtered, or perhaps Ultan will have killed a deer, and we can have a huge *fulacht* in the field above the beach and glut ourselves on venison and Gobnat can make her famous raspberry pudding – I'm sure there are raspberries still in the woods, it's not Lunasa yet – and Eva and I will serve the gallant Romans with bowls of yellow cream from my father's herds scented with rose petals and sweetened with honey, and I shall wear my golden torc and Eva can wear hers, and we shall be like young goddesses and our hair will glisten in the firelight and the Romans will want to marry us, and we shall say, Never! She laughed, threw herself onto her back and flung her arms out and almost cried 'Never!' aloud.

Suddenly, she sat up. She thought she could hear sounds in the distance. Ultan, returning from his cattle-buying expedition! Could it be? Ye gods, please let it be Ultan! If it were, they'd all be saved. Ultan was the finest warrior in the land, and the bravest, everyone said so. He had slain several of his enemies in one-to-one combat and the neighbouring tribes were in thrall to him. Ultan would know what to do.

Filled with a burst of new energy, Sun´va sprang to her feet and ran towards the sound, which was coming north along the cattle trail. As she ran, the consternation of sounds became clamorous on the sweltering air, the rumble and ruckle of carts, the bass hum of cattle lowing. Now she could hear dogs yelping, men swearing at the beasts. And at last, Ultan emerged out of the noise and dust, towering over them all, astride the frontboard of his cart, the reins held high to his breastbone and his *brat* flying in the breeze, whipped up by the speed of his own approach. His beard was caked with the dust and sweat of the journey, his bronze curls were raked into damp spikes, his face streaked, his tunic tattered and his trousers spattered and ripped. His hound, Duvagaun, also caked with dirt, stood up in the back of the cart and raised heaven with his excited barking at the approach to home.

'Come and help, daughter, help with the horses,' called Ultan, without greeting Sun´va, over the noise. He ran his hands through his hair, making it stick up more than ever. 'And what are you doing in that short little tunic? Climbing trees again, no doubt. You're a *spailpín*, you are, Sun´va daughter of Ultan, showing your knees like that. Can you not dress like a lady now that you're grown? No one will marry you if you behave like a slave boy.'

Sun´va pulled half-heartedly at the girdle she wore around her waist, to loosen the fabric of her tunic so that it would hang down and cover her knees, but she answered her father breathlessly, 'Father, listen, I have news. Momentous news!'

The farmhands were coming running from the fields now to help herd the new cattle that thundered behind him.

But Ultan was tired from his journey, and couldn't believe that Sun´va's news was of any great import. 'Come, daughter, and kiss your father, home from a long, hard journey,' he said, opening his arms to Sun´va.

'Father, father,' said Sun´va, 'there's no time for that. You must go down to the beach at once, and take the men with you. The Romans are coming from the east.'

'The Romans, by Daghdha! How do you know they are Romans?'

'I saw them, from the oak tree at the cliff. Three ships. Not a quarter of an hour ago, they were just visible on the horizon. They won't have come ashore yet. We'll have to fight them, Ultan, won't we? We can't be invaded by Romans! They'll enslave us. They'll steal our cattle, lay waste our land, they'll – they'll marry Eva!'

She had no intention of being married herself, even though her father told her it was a woman's destiny.

'Steady, steady, daughter, and tell me what you saw, precisely.'

Sun´va closed her eyes and babbled, 'Three ships, big ones, huge, and moving swiftly.'

'Well, daughter, I will come with you to the shore,' said Ultan, 'and we will see these Romans of yours. Will that suit you?'

'Yes.' Sun´va smiled. 'But now, we'll go now, we must go immediately, come on, there's no time to lose.'

Without waiting for an answer, Sun´va turned on her

heel and started to run back towards the strand. Ultan followed with long, rapid strides.

'What'll we do, father?' she asked, as they stood together on the cliff by Sun´va's curiosity tree, looking out to sea. The Roman ships were easily visible now, and they were making good progress.

'Well,' said Ultan, thinking quickly, his eyebrows arched with concentration, 'it's not a real raid. There's only three boats. They don't mean to do battle.'

'But we can't just let them land, can we, Ultan? We must fight them off!'

'You're right,' said Ultan, 'we must fight them off, for whatever reason they come. But we can't muster an army within hours. We'll send out the messengers immediately to the neighbouring *tuatha* to summon my kinsmen and their clients and friends to battle. But they won't be here before the ships land, so in the meantime we are going to have to stall the Romans.'

'But all we have to call on are the farmhands,' said Sun´va. 'And the cattle-slaves you brought from the south.'

'So what we need to do is this,' said Ultan. 'We'll get everyone down to the beach – slaves, women, farmhands, artisans, everyone, horses, chariots, farm-carts, every movable stick we own, the cattle even can form a back line, to fill out the crowd.'

'Father! You're not going to fight the Roman army with a herd of cattle and a handful of slaves?'

'Of course we're not going to fight them, not yet, because we can't, but I have a plan. We'll give them a right riotous welcome that'll scare them half to death. We have to give the impression of hundreds, thousands, of angry warriors, seething with bloodlust and bursting to rip them to pieces and hang their filthy Roman guts out to dry on Irish rocks.'

'Oh, Ultan!' Sun´va breathed, feeling herself going pale. 'That's horrible.'

'Good!' said Ultan with a short laugh. 'Even you were taken in for a moment. Now all we have to do is convince the Romans likewise, and we can at least gain a few hours, maybe even a few days, give ourselves the time to gather what forces we can.'

'We'll need a trumpeter,' Ultan continued. 'We must have a trumpeter to help create a *ruaille buaille*. That can be your job, Sun´va. But first, go and get the womenfolk together – where in the name of all the gods are they anyway?'

'Within doors, I'm sure, in the shade. It's too hot for working in the fields.'

'Well, find them, and tell them to come, every woman of them, to the shore, to form the second line. I'll see to the men and the animals, and I'll send runners to call the troops.'

'Yes, father,' said Sun´va, and she started to break immediately into a run.

'Sun´va! Come back. I have something to tell you, my daughter, that you will have to warn the women about.'

Sun´va stopped in her tracks and looked back at her father.

'It's … ah, a matter of some … delicacy.'

'Delicacy?' Sun´va was puzzled. This wasn't the sort of word Ultan normally used.

Ultan circled his daughter's slender wrist with his

fingers and drew her close. She wrinkled her nose at the stink of his body after hours on the road, but she soon forgot her discomfort as she listened to what he whispered.

'Ultan! Oh, father! Oh, Eva will die!'

'I knew I should have married you both off before you turned fourteen. You're going wild on me, you one way and Eva another. Just tell Eva it doesn't matter. They're only slaves. It's nothing, just a war tactic. And well done, my child. Your curiosity may well have saved your people. But there is no time to lose. Go now, quick, explain it to the women. I rely on you, Sun´va, to get them all here, fast, and I don't want anybody fainting or sniggering. I just want concentrated bodies here, and voices. I want everyone hullooing and yelling at the tops of their voices. Oh yes, and the trumpet. Don't forget. I put you in charge of the trumpet. Get away with you now, as fast as you can, daughter, and do as I say, do you hear me now?'

'Yes, father,' said Sun´va, her voice swollen with pride, excitement and fear.

Then she turned from him and fled. Every time she thought of what he had said, what she had to explain to the women, giggles rose in her like air bubbles as she ran. They were giving her a stitch in her side.

CHAPTER 3

Well, well, thou hast a careful father, child
Romeo & Juliet Act 3, Sc v

'I wish those Phillips people had never left the neighbour-hood.'

Ray Quinn seemed to be speaking to the property section of the newspaper.

'You're not allowed to read at table, Dad,' said Julia, reaching for the marmalade with a jangle of bangles. 'Can't reach it,' she added. 'Could you pass the marmalade, please, Dad?'

'Why?' asked Lydia. 'Why do you wish …'

'It's my house, Julia,' said Ray, lowering the newspaper. 'I make the rules.'

'No, you don't,' argued Julia. 'That's dictatorship and that's not allowed. This family is a democracy, isn't it, Mum? And you still haven't passed the marmalade, Dad.'

'Even in a democracy,' said her mother, 'under-eighteens don't have a vote, Julia. And it's *our* house, Ray.'

'Why do you wish the Phillipses hadn't left?' asked Lydia again. She reached around her father's newspaper and secured the marmalade for her sister. 'You never much liked that family. They had three cars and took up all the parking spaces. You always hated that. And remember that awful strimmer thing they had, gave us all a headache.'

'Well, at least they were a family.'

'Oh yes, a *family*,' said Julia sarcastically, jabbing her toast with her marmalady knife. 'We all love families, don't we? Two up, two down, perfect, just like us. So who's moving in? A drug baron? A member of Fianna Fáil? A *Single Parent*?'

Lydia giggled. Ray glared at her.

'A bicycle shop,' said Ray.

'A bicycle shop! Well, *that* sounds fun, doesn't it, Lyd? Cheer up, Dad, it might have been a casino. Or a brothel.'

'This is a *residential* area, Julia. Oh yes, turn up your nose, young lady, very fetching that is, most attractive, I must say, especially since you got that nose ring. You look like a prize bull.'

'I do not,' said Julia. She was used to this line of insults. She didn't take it seriously. That's just how parents were. Couldn't cope with their children growing up. Felt threatened, that was their problem. Knew they were going to be booted upstairs soon to the oldies department, while the youngsters took over and started to run the show. Sad, really.

'Bulls have rings *through* their noses,' she explained carefully for the umpteenth time. 'I haven't got a ring through my nose, Dad. That's called having your septum pierced. It's extremely painful and, I agree with you, also quite unattractive. A discreet stud in the nostril is quite a different thing. Now, can we get back to the bicycles, please, Dad? Trring-trring?'

'It says here that the "Wheel of Life" bicycle company has bought the house next door for an undisclosed sum and is about to fit it out as a shop.'

'Wheel of *Life*?' squeaked Julia. 'Well, we can't have that, can we? Hippies, obviously. Crusties, I have no doubt. People with dogs and dreadlocks. Dogs *with* dreadlocks, even. Dear, oh dear, oh dearie me.' She was enjoying herself hugely.

'And tattoos,' added Lydia slyly, joining in the teasing. Her dad hated tattoos. 'You forgot tattoos.'

'Oh, I don't think they'd bother tattooing their dogs,' said Julia with a giggle. 'Bit of a waste of effort, wouldn't you say, Dad?'

Ray put the newspaper down with a sigh and looked despairingly at his two daughters, who were shaking with silent laughter.

'When I was your age …' he began.

Julia stood up and made a great sweeping movement with an imaginary bow across the strings of an imaginary violin.

Lydia clapped. 'Beethoven, my favourite.' She always picked up Julia's mood when she was like this, teasing and light-hearted, and they made a double act that drove their parents wild. 'Romance number two?'

'Exactly,' said Julia, sitting down again. 'Number two. That's just what Dad talks. Lots of number two. You were saying, Dad?'

'I was saying that it's time you two started to grow up and

understand the value of money. Goodness knows you're well able to spend it. A bicycle shop next door will bring down the value of this very nice house of ours, your inheritance, I might add.'

'That'll be the day,' said Julia. 'We're heiresses, Lydia. And how much are the mortgage repayments, did you say, Dad?'

'You may laugh …' their father went on.

'Thank you,' said Julia. 'Ho-ho-ho.'

'You are impossible,' said Ray, shaking his head in mock despair. 'I'm going to work. Somebody has to bring home the bacon around here.'

Ray kissed Frankie swiftly and slapped both daughters lightly on the upper arms.

'Love you all,' he said, picking up his car keys, 'though I can't imagine why. Bye.'

'Unconditional love, it's called,' Julia shouted after him. 'Parents just *do* it.'

CHAPTER 4

Under love's heavy burden do I sink
Romeo & Juliet Act 1, Sc iv

'Julia?' said Lydia, as they stood together after breakfast at the sink. Julia washed; Lydia dried. They'd always done it that way, since they were tiny. Even as toddlers, Julia had got to play with the suds, while Lydia fussed about with a tea towel, mopping up.

'Hmm?' said Julia, blowing up under a tiny, escaping detergent bubble to keep it in the air.

'It's about Jonathan,' said Lydia, holding a half-dried plate up in front of her neatly buttoned cardigan, like a breastplate. 'Watch it, by the way, your sleeve's dipping in the water.'

'Jonathan?' said Julia dreamily, changing her mind and bursting the bubble. 'Jonathan Who?' She pushed her trailing sleeves up above her elbow.

Lydia wasn't going to be distracted now that she'd decided to tell.

'Jonathan Walker,' she said. 'I met him yesterday. I wanted you to know.'

'Lucky you,' said Julia, sarcastically. She swished her brush around, moving a wispy hillock of suds to one side of the washing-up basin, and started to scrub dried-in fragments of cornflakes off a cereal bowl.

'I mean, I met him by *arrangement*,' said Lydia softly.

'What?' asked Julia, still concentrating, apparently, on the bowl. 'You mean you had an *appointment* with him?'

'You make him sound like a dentist,' said Lydia, attempting a joke.

'Well, I didn't think you meant a *date*, as Mum would say,' said Julia, turning to look at her sister. 'You don't do "dates", do you, Lydia?'

Lydia felt the blood rushing to her face again. Why *didn't* she 'do dates'? How come she'd never had a boyfriend and Julia'd had several?

'Well …' she said.

'Lydia! You don't mean to say you're going *out* with that thug Jonathan Walker!'

'N-no,' said Lydia. 'Not exactly. We just met for a cup of coffee. And he's not a thug, Julia. He's a bit full of himself, but he's … kind of sweet too, in a way. He was nice to me.'

'A law-tay?' Julia couldn't get enough venom into her voice. She didn't think the 'kind of sweet' was even worth arguing about. 'Is that what you had?'

'Yeah,' said Lydia, innocently. 'In that coffee shop, down by the harbour, you know the …'

'Jonathan Walker took *you* to that glitzy place? That's where *I* used to go with him!'

'Why shouldn't he?' said Lydia, holding her breastplate

more fiercely to her.

'No reason,' said Julia airily, viciously. 'I suppose it makes a sort of twisted sense, really.'

'What do you mean?'

'I mean, you are my identical twin, Lydia.'

'Well, thank you for sharing that with me,' said Lydia, attempting to emulate Julia's sarcastic tone. 'I had noticed, though.'

'Don't be like that,' said Julia wearily. 'But clearly — now, Lydia, I don't mean to be hurtful — but clearly, you are a substitute for me.'

'Don't be ridiculous,' said Lydia, outraged. 'I'm completely different from you.'

But of course she *wasn't* completely different. She was only partly different. That was the whole problem. When they were children and went everywhere together, dressed to match, holding hands, Lydia had thought of herself as Julia's shadow. Julia was the bright, capable, outgoing, smiling one; Lydia was the grey, faithful, secretive, silent one. She didn't mind. It was nice to have a bright, out-going one to shield her from the onslaughts of the world. But now they were growing up, and Julia was busy becoming just Julia. How come Lydia went on being only Julia's twin?

'But you *look* exactly like me,' said Julia. 'And for a shallow person like Jonathan, that's about all that counts. He was always going on about my hair, my eyes, my skin, always wanted to tell me what sort of make-up I should wear. He's obsessed with appearance. Good-looking people often are. And we are pretty, you know, Lydia. Not bad, anyway. We're practically blonde.'

'Well, thanks for the "we",' muttered Lydia. 'But we're not blonde. And Jonathan's not shallow. That's not fair.'

'Strawberry blonde then,' Julia insisted. 'So it's obvious,' she continued. 'He wants me back, but is afraid to ask, after the way he treated me, so he's making do with you instead. Shallow, see?'

'*Making do*!' Lydia put down the plate she'd been holding, very carefully, because if she didn't concentrate, she was afraid she'd smash it. 'Making do with *me*! You are suggesting that I am some sort of second-rate version of you! I always knew you were an arrogant cow, Julia Quinn, but this takes the biscuit, this absolutely takes the flaming cream cracker!'

Lydia was shaking, but only partly with anger. She was also shaking with the effort of telling Julia about her assignation with Jonathan, and with a kind of mute rage, too, at Jonathan, because now that Julia pointed it out, that was obviously what was going on. She *was* being used as a sort of ersatz – instant Julia, just add sparkle – or, worse, as a way for Jonathan to winkle his way back in with Julia.

'Sorry, sorry,' said Julia. 'Sorry, I didn't mean it like that. Don't get your knickers in a twist.'

Lydia took a deep breath. Now she came to think of it,

Jonathan had behaved oddly yesterday. He'd invited her for coffee, but he'd seemed distracted, talked about the weather, asked about Julia, talked about his school report, asked what sort of report Julia'd got, talked about rugby (rugby! – surely it was obvious that Lydia hadn't the remotest interest in rugby), mentioned Julia yet again. She hadn't noticed much at the time, but yes, it had been Julia, Julia, Julia. Hadn't it? She blushed again to think that she'd thought he was interested in *her*. Though he had tried to kiss her, definitely he had, as they parted. She'd got such a surprise, she'd turned her head and deflected it into a peck on the cheek.

'OK,' she said, with a sigh. 'I'm sorry too.'

'Are you meeting him again?' Julia asked, more gently now.

'Eh – no,' said Lydia. He hadn't suggested it and she hadn't had the nerve to either. 'That proves it, doesn't it?' she added sadly.

'No,' said Julia, though really she thought it did. 'Not nece-celery.'

Lydia managed a smile. She was nearly nine before she'd learnt to say the word 'necessarily' properly, and her mispronunciation had become a family joke. But though she didn't want to fight with Julia, especially not over – let's face it, she said to herself – a thug like Jonathan Walker, she was smarting in a place she couldn't put a name on.

CHAPTER 5

Two households, both alike in dignity
Romeo & Juliet Prologue

The Residents' Association took Ray's view of the proposed bicycle shop and had it shut down before it even opened. There were shops across the road from their house: a rip-off convenience store, a dusty hardware shop that sold wilting bedding plants that Frankie would buy out of pity, to rescue them from certain death, a chemist's and a dry-cleaner's. This meant that it was hard to argue on residential-area grounds, but they were able to make some sort of argument to do with loading and unloading and the clearway and bus lane that ran past their house. Ray had always grumbled about the clearway in the past, but he was glad of it now.

'What, no hippies?' asked Julia with mock disappointment. 'Not even a few muscley mechanics with oily rags hanging out of their pockets and smelling of tyre-rubber? Aw, Dad! I could have done with one of those.'

'No hippies,' said Ray smugly. 'No muscle-men. You see, *there's* the power of collective action. You girls can learn from this. Local democracy, it's called.'

'And what is the Residents' Association's view on black people?' asked Julia, looking out of the front window.

'What are you *talking* about, Julia? Black people? What have black people got to do with bicycle shops?'

'Dunno,' said Julia, 'only there are two, no, three, no, *five*, walking up the garden path next door, not counting the littl'uns.'

'*What!*' Ray sprang to his feet and ran to the window.

'But it's OK, Dad, they haven't got a bicycle between them. Just a buggy, two buggies, eh, *three* buggies and an awful lot of suitcases, and, let me see, a rucksack and, oh yes, dreadlocks, some of them, or at least, little teeny-weeny plaits, and *gorgeous* clothes, but no dogs, no, definitely no dogs. Well, that's a relief. Dogs make *such* bad neighbours. Always poohing on the pavement and barking in the night.'

'Oh my God!' groaned Ray.

'Have you got a problem, Dad?'

'Oh sweet, suffering saviour,' said Ray.

'Very colourful turn of phrase, that, Dad,' said Julia. 'Though I think that counts as swearing, you know, blasphemy. Mum doesn't like it.'

'Holy mother of …'

'Ah-ah. Just stop, now, Dad. I think they look … *interesting*. Oh look, Lydia, there's one our sort of age. He's … did I say "interesting"? Could I revise that upwards, please?'

'Hmm,' said Lydia, peering over Julia's shoulder at a tall

young African, maybe a few years older than themselves, who was halfway up the garden path next door. He had a small child on his shoulders and he was twisting his neck so he could talk up to the little fellow, who was tweaking his ears. 'I see what you mean,' she said. 'Yes, I think "interesting" might be an understatement all right.'

'It's a hostel,' sobbed Ray from between the fingers of both hands, which he had stretched across his face. 'They're turning it into a bleeding *hostel*. Next door to *us*. It's an invasion, that's what it is. What did we do to deserve this?'

'Objected to having a bicycle shop there,' said Julia matter-of-factly. 'Well, Dad, that's local democracy for you!'

'There'll be goats in the garden, you mark my words,' said Ray darkly.

'Goats in the garden! Da-a-ad!'

'They eat goats in Africa. I'm not making this up.'

'*We* eat *cows*, Dad,' said Julia, with heavy patience. 'And is our garden full of cows? I mean, hello?'

'Anyway,' Lydia chipped in, 'that garden could do with a goat or two. It's a jungle.'

'A *jungle*!' spat Ray. 'Huh!'

The Curiosity Tree 2

'**D**uvagaun! Duvagaun! Duvagaun!'

From his position at the front of the assembled Celts, right at the edge of the water, Ultan roared for his dog. This was the signal for the slave at the very back of the motley crowd to release the dog into the herd of over-excited, panic-stricken cattle.

As Duvagaun raced towards his master's voice, yelping and snarling at cattle that got in his way, every other dog in the neighbourhood was also released, and the squealing, barking pack raced through the lines of cattle, who picked up their hooves in a crazy, heavy-footed, manic dance of terror. Crazed by the dogs yelping at their ankles, the cattle charged down the dunes towards the sea, slithering and sliding in their own squirting shit, and bellowing with rage and fear. The sheep, which were gathered in a bobbing woolly mass in front of them, were forced to race in all directions in their panicky efforts to escape the wall of cattle-flesh that was falling in on top of them. With bleating sheep darting among them, the next line, of horsemen and charioteers (in reality slaves and ploughboys), galloped forward towards the women, who were dressed in men's trousers as a disguise and were bashing cauldron lids and rattling spoons and ladles and letting bloodcurdling yodels. The line of women and children parted to let the horsemen through, and the animals pranced and neighed and pawed the air at the edge of the sea.

From her branch in the curiosity tree, Sun´va could see the almighty commotion her father's plan had created, and she joined in with every breath in her body, bellowing into the war trumpet she held to her lips until bright and wriggling tadpoles swam across her vision from light-headedness. The din was so fearsome that you couldn't make out any individual sounds, apart from the soaring sound of the trumpet, and there was sand everywhere in the air, so that you couldn't see a thing, only smell and feel your way. Even from her tree, Sun´va could easily believe there were hundreds of fighting men charging into battle, though she knew perfectly well there were only about fifteen or twenty armed men, a handful on horseback, and the rest of the 'force' was made up of women and children and farm animals.

Beyond the sand clouds and mêlée on the beach, she could see her father at the head of the line of menfolk, striding towards the water. It was important not to giggle if she was to keep up the trumpeting, but it was hard not to laugh at the sight of the farmhands marching forward as if into battle, their spines straight and knobbly, their shoulders thrown back and their buttocks and haunches clenched and muscular. For the handful of men that Ultan had mustered and put at the head of the attack were stark naked – they hadn't a stitch between them.

'The idea is to shock the enemy,' Ultan had explained. 'It dismays them and stops them in their tracks. It makes them think they are dealing with savages who will stop at nothing. The effect doesn't last, of course. They recover quick enough, but even that short delay gives us an advantage.'

The naked warriors reached the water and started to splash into the shallows. They were yodelling and roaring at the tops of their voices. Their bright hair was wild and matted about their enormous heads and their huge bodies gleamed white in the sunshine. They brandished their swords and waved their shields high over their heads, leaving their torsos and their vulnerable private parts unprotected.

Ultan was moving away from his men, now, and was advancing towards the Romans in their ships, through the waves, leaving his band of naked warriors behind him, with their shields and swords lowered. He waved his sword in the air and hullooed to catch their attention.

When he was sure they were all watching him, he raised his great leather shield over his head, spun it around and then flung it into the water, where it landed with a slap and a splash, and bobbed about, well out of his reach. Then he spun his sword around in the air and flung that also. It disappeared under the water, leaving him, apart from his hair, naked as the day he was born, up to his thighs in the sea, and with his arms thrown open as if he wanted to embrace the world. He waded forward a few steps further and, bringing his hands up to cup his mouth to form a megaphone, he shouted a greeting to the invaders.

The Romans had no notion what he was calling, but his gestures looked friendly. It really did look – could it be true? – as if he were welcoming them ashore.

Ultan shouted a welcome to them again, this time with his arms raised to the sky.

One Roman, at the front of the leading ship, raised his own sword and shield, as if he were about to leap overboard and meet Ultan in single combat. Sun´va held her breath as she watched the slow movements of his arms.

Then he shouted an order over his shoulder, and, turning back to Ultan, threw his sword and shield overboard with a slap and a splash, in the same gesture of submission and friendship that the Irish chieftain had used.

The Roman raised his arms then, again copying Ultan's gesture, and for a moment time seemed to stand still, the naked man in the water with his arms raised, calling greetings, and the Roman centurion in full battledress with his arms raised in the same gesture, returning his greeting: 'Ave!'

As soon as he was sure he had gained the Romans' trust, at least for the moment, Ultan turned quickly and yelled orders to the men at the edge of the water.

'Away with you, quick,' he roared at them, for of course the Romans couldn't understand a word he said to his own people. 'Move everyone up the beach and away out of sight. Quick, quick. I don't want them to see that our army is only women and children and cattle. Quick now, disperse! Fly! Be gone!'

Then he turned to the Romans again with a beatific smile and bowed low in the water. As he raised his head, he made beckoning gestures with his arms and turned away from them towards the beach, still beckoning widely with his arms, as if he were hauling in their boats with a giant, invisible net. He was like a great, streaming, naked sea-god welcoming home a fishing fleet.

'Row in!' yelled the centurion to his men. 'We'll take him at his word. Beach the boats!'

CHAPTER 6

From ancient grudge break to new mutiny
Romeo & Juliet Prologue

The noise woke Julia and Lydia up. Even from the back of the house they could hear the din.

They tumbled downstairs and into the sitting room to see what was going on. Eight o'clock in the morning, and the road was full of honking cars. Pedestrians thronged the roadway, infuriating drivers who were trying to inch their way through to work. The traffic lights changed from red to green to red again and not a single car got through. Women swarmed over the pavement, bashing dustbin lids with wooden spoons and ladles. Someone with a megaphone had half-scaled a lamp-post and was screeching so raucously into it that nobody could hear what they were shouting. The racket was tremendous. The twins retreated to the kitchen to get away from it.

Frankie sat at the kitchen table, her head in her hands.

'What's going on, Mum?' asked Lydia.

'Protest,' said Frankie, not raising her head.

'Against the hostel?'

'Of course.'

'Those people are never our Residents' Association?'

'I think it's rent-a-crowd,' said Frankie.

'Rent-a-bigot, more like,' said Julia.

'Rent-a-crowda-bigots,' said Lydia, with a hysterical edge to her voice.

'Dad has nothing to do with this, has he, Mum?' asked Julia.

Frankie didn't answer.

'Mum, where's Dad?' said Lydia. 'Mum?'

'Don't know,' said Frankie with a sigh. 'Gone to work, I suppose. I slept in. I didn't hear him leave.'

'I'm going to call the guards,' said Lydia.

'I've already done that,' said Frankie. 'Half an hour ago. They haven't come yet. It's been on "Morning Ireland". On the traffic report part I mean, not the news.'

A knock came to the back door. Frankie started.

'Let's not answer it,' said Lydia. 'It's probably one of them, the protesters.'

'Maybe it's the guards,' said Julia.

'Don't be silly,' said Frankie. 'Why would the guards come around the back?'

'Well, then, it might be a reporter,' said Julia. 'You know, one of the *paparazzi*. We might be on telly.'

The knock came again, timid but persistent.

'Maybe it's one of *them*,' said Julia. 'The bl–, the people next door. Oh, maybe it's your man, the tall one. I'll open it.'

'I think I'd better,' said Frankie. She stood up.

The twins watched her, ready to spring to her defence if it were a spill-over from the protest outside.

Frankie opened the door a crack, and the girls could hear a soft voice outside. After a moment, Frankie stood back and opened the door wide. A young black woman in a long, spectacularly patterned cotton dress and flat leather sandals stepped in nervously. She turned to close the door after her, and they could see a sleeping baby, tiny and curly-headed with gleaming skin, as if somebody had polished it up, wrapped tightly in a fold of her dress, with its little flat nose pressed against the woman's back.

'Aw,' they both said together, gazing in delight at the child. They didn't go in much for babies, but this one looked so sweet, all swaddled up and sleeping, his head like a furry chestnut in the folds of his mother's dress.

The woman smiled. 'He's two weeks old,' she said, in English too perfectly articulated to be her first language. 'His name is Patrick.'

'Patrick!'

'We called him for Ireland.'

'Aw,' they said again, and smiled foolishly.

'I thought the noise might wake him up,' said Patrick's mother, indicating the front of the house, 'but he likes his sleep.'

She turned to Frankie and asked if she could borrow some milk for her children's breakfast. They had all been awake for ages with the noise and were very frightened. She thought if she could give them their cornflakes, that might distract them for a while, but she couldn't get through the mob to the shop.

'Of course,' said Frankie, swinging open the fridge door. 'We always have loads of milk. I'm always buying too much, actually, and then I have to make puddings to use it all up. Take a litre. Take *two*.'

'If you're sure,' said their neighbour.

'Yes, yes,' said Frankie, 'of course I'm sure.'

'I'll replace it later, when the crowds go away.'

'Oh, don't bother, as I say, I always …' Frankie was babbling, embarrassed that this woman should be prevented from getting milk for her children by Irish people behaving like Nazis in the street.

'I will replace it,' said the other woman gravely. 'I do not come begging.'

'Of *course* not,' said Frankie, blushing bright red. 'I didn't mean …'

'My name is Catherine,' said the woman with the baby, and offered her hand.

'Frankie,' said Frankie, grasping her hand with too much enthusiasm. 'So pleased to meet you. And these are my daughters, Julia and Lydia.'

Julia and Lydia stepped forward to shake hands. Catherine's small hand was cool and dry and her skin felt somehow brittle, like autumn leaves.

'Twins,' said Catherine. 'That is good luck.'

'Oh?' said Frankie. 'Is it?'

'In my country …' said Catherine.

'Which is?' said Frankie, eagerly.

'Far away,' Catherine answered evasively, not meeting her eyes. 'Goodbye, Mrs Frankie. Thank you. I see you later with the milk. Two litres.'

Catherine raised one hand and twinkled her fingers at Julia and Lydia, and then she was gone.

'Well!' said Julia.

'Patrick!' said Lydia. 'Dad'll *die*!'

'Oh Lydia!' said Frankie. 'Those poor people, it's all so *awful*.'

CHAPTER 7

How cam'st thou hither, tell me, and wherefore?
Romeo & Juliet Act 2, Sc ii

It was on the news that evening about the race riot in their street. Two people had been arrested and an injunction had been taken out against a group of activists – not the local Residents' Association, as it turned out. In fact, the chairman of the Residents' Association came on the radio, anxious to wash his hands of the whole affair.

'That's right,' said Ray, nodding, as the Residents' Association man spoke. 'Of course it wasn't a race riot!'

'How do you know what it was, Dad?' argued Julia. 'You weren't even here. It was awful. Those poor people were trapped in their house. Their children were hungry. There's a baby next door, you know.'

'Don't exaggerate, Julia,' said Frankie. 'They just ran out of milk. You make it sound like a famine.'

'People around here don't go in for race riots,' said Ray steadily. 'That much I do know.'

'People around here,' Julia mimicked. 'Oh yes, nice, gleaming, fresh-faced *white* people with mortgages and lawnmowers, people like us.'

'There's nothing wrong with people like us,' Ray retorted.

They were interrupted by a ring at the doorbell. Frankie turned to Lydia and said, 'You go, you're the calmest, there's a love.'

'Don't let them in if they're black!' Julia shouted sarcastically after her. 'We'd never be able to sell the house if we did that! We'd get a reputation.'

'Hush, Julia,' said Frankie.

'I never said anything like that,' said Ray in an unnaturally quiet voice. 'You are putting words into my mouth. I have nothing against black people.'

'As long as they are in Africa,' said Julia.

'I didn't *say* that,' said Ray in a suppressed shout.

'But you think it.'

'I *don't* think it! How do you know what I think?'

'Well, then,' said Julia, 'what's your problem?'

Ray sighed. 'I've told you. I've explained till the cows come home about the value of property. I don't care what colour anyone is, but I don't want to live beside a hostel, that's all.'

'Shh,' urged Frankie. 'Lydia's opened the door.'

They all stopped for a moment and listened to what was happening in the hall.

'Oh, thank you,' Lydia was saying. 'It's kind of you to … You didn't need to …'

They couldn't hear what the other person said.

'What is it?' they heard Lydia say then. 'A *love* bean! What's that? Do you eat it?'

Again there came a muffled reply and then they could hear Lydia's voice rippling with laughter. 'You'll have to show it to her yourself. I couldn't remember all that. Come in, come in!'

'Oh no!' said Ray. 'Trust Lydia to go inviting some damned stranger in when we're eating our dinner. Has she no tact?'

'Ray! Shh, they'll hear you. And we've finished eating, it's all right.'

The kitchen door opened, and a young man, tall and rather thin and very, very black, filled the doorway. It was the boy that Lydia and Julia had seen from the window the previous day, with a child on his shoulders. He was alone now, dressed in faded jeans and a long, light-coloured V-necked cotton sweater over a T-shirt. A plastic carrier bag jostled awkwardly at his knees.

Lydia's voice came from behind him. 'Go on in,' she was saying, 'they won't bite you.'

The young man stepped forward, into the room, ducking his head, the typical defensive gesture of a tall person used to doorways with low lintels.

'I am returning the milk, Mrs Frankie,' he said, raising the bag and pointing at it. The geometric outline of two blue litre cartons was clearly visible through the milky plastic, and one sharp corner had already poked its way through the flimsy bag.

'Oh, thank you,' said Frankie, standing up and taking the bag from the young man.

'Mrs Frankie!' spluttered Ray, staring first at the young man and then at his wife. Frankie resolutely refused to meet his eye. 'Have you two met before?'

Nobody answered him.

'This is Tito,' said Lydia's head, appearing around Tito's body in the doorway. 'He lives next door, you know. Catherine sent him.'

'Catherine?' said Ray, mystified.

Nobody enlightened him.

'She said you must have this,' Tito went on, holding out his fist. 'To thank you for your great kindness.'

'It was nothing, I don't need thanking,' said Frankie, flustered, her hands twisting nervously. She chanced a flicker of an eye in Ray's direction. His knife and fork, clenched in his fists, were pointing at the ceiling.

'Put down your cutlery,' Frankie hissed.

'Show her, Tito,' said Lydia.

Tito turned his fist over, and delicately opened his long fingers, one by one. Sitting in the middle of his pinkish palm lay what looked like a polished and gleaming chestnut.

'It's an African love bean,' said Lydia. 'It's a token of l–' She looked at her father. 'Friendship,' she amended. 'You give it to someone you want to … make a friend of.'

'Catherine said I should give it to you, Mrs Frankie,' Tito explained again, 'from her. To say thank you for being such a good neighbour today.'

Frankie held out her hand, and Tito tipped the love bean

onto her palm. Frankie rolled it between her fingers.

'Is Catherine your sister?' Julia asked.

Tito laughed and looked at Julia for the first time.

'Who is Catherine?' Ray asked.

Still nobody answered him.

'My sister! No. I never met her before last week. We don't even speak the same language. They just put us together because we are all from Africa. There must be people from three or four countries in there.' He nodded towards the house next door.

'Is it really a bean?' Frankie asked, looking at the strange object.

'I don't think so,' said Tito. 'But it is some sort of seed, I believe. They come ashore in my country. People say they come from the Caribbean, on the tide, I don't know. Anyway, the people pick them up off the beaches. It is good luck to find one, because they are not common. I don't think you can eat them, but people like them because they are so beautiful. And so ... not common?'

'Rare,' said Julia.

'Rare,' he said, 'yes, rare.'

'Beautiful,' said Frankie. 'Oh, yes, it is beautiful. Thank you. I shall ... put it here.' She laid the large brown seed on the windowsill and its satiny mahogany surface gleamed richly against the white- painted woodwork.

'Is it a love token?' Julia asked.

Tito laughed again, and his eyes gleamed like two love beans in his head, dark and deep, glossy and mysterious.

'Well, people say that, but maybe it is just some nonsense for the tourists,' he said. 'But it's a nice idea. There are worse traditions.' His voice was very melodious and, like Catherine, he articulated his words with exaggerated precision, his pale tongue flickering in his mouth as he enunciated his consonants. He went suddenly serious. 'Much worse,' he muttered, so quietly that he could scarcely be heard.

'Well, thank you, Tito,' said Frankie. 'And please thank Catherine for me. Would you like some coffee?'

Ray spluttered again. He reached for a tissue from the box behind him on the fridge.

"Scuse me,' he muttered, wiping his mouth. 'Something went down the wrong way, I think.'

'Oh dear,' said Julia, with mock sympathy. 'Finding something hard to swallow, Dad?'

Ray glared at her and shook his head.

'I don't think I will stay for coffee,' said Tito. 'They need help at home with the children. They are very unsettled. It's hard to get them to sleep in a strange place. They hate the noise.'

'What noise?' asked Ray.

Tito smiled. 'Traffic,' he said with a shrug. 'We come from a very different sort of place.'

'What sort of place?' asked Julia, desperate to keep him

talking. She just wanted to hear that melodious sound going on and on.

'Hot,' said Tito. 'Bright all day with yellow sunshine. The earth is dust, the people poor. They sing. At night the stars are sharp. It is three miles to the water source. Babies die. The flies make a buzzing noise and there is always something howling in the trees. The women wear bright dresses.' He stopped as suddenly as he had started, and shrugged again. 'Different,' he said. 'Goodbye now, and again thank you for the milk.'

He stretched out a hand to Frankie, and she shook it warmly. He considered Ray for a moment, and finally offered him his hand. Sheepishly, Ray took it and shook it briefly.

'Goodbye, Libya,' said Tito. 'Goodbye, Libya's double.'

'Julia!' Julia stood up and shot her hand out. 'I'm Julia. She's Lydia. We're twins.'

'Really?' said Tito, and grinned at her, but he took her hand and shook it solemnly.

'Goodbye,' he said again.

And he was gone. Seconds later, they heard the click of the front door. There was silence for a moment in the kitchen.

'Oh my God!' said Julia at last. 'Oh my God, what a …!'

Ray glared at her. Julia's unfinished sentence hung for a moment in the air between them, suspended between their two wills, his stare seeming to dare her to finish.

But it was Lydia who dared. 'What a *smasher*!' she said, and the tension broke. Everyone laughed, because it was their mother's old-fashioned word and it sounded absurd coming from Lydia.

'And the way he *talks*!' said Julia, casting caution onto the dispersing wave of tension. 'He's so *different*. "The earth is dust, the people sing." And, oh Mum, "Mrs Frankie"! Doesn't it make you feel ... all *special* when he says that?'

'I can't say it does,' said Frankie dryly.

Ray stomped out of the kitchen. Nobody noticed.

'I saw him first,' Julia said as they cleared the table after dinner, 'yesterday, on the garden path. I pointed him out to you. I'm entitled. It's fate, Lydia, it's written in the stars. He's mine.'

'I *met* him first,' Lydia countered. 'I opened the door to him. I practically introduced him to you. You could have opened the door if you hadn't been so busy arguing with Dad. But you didn't, I did. Anyway, he likes me, I can tell.'

She flicked her hair over her shoulder, with a gesture she'd seen Julia use a thousand times, but which Lydia had never before had the nerve to use herself. It meant, There's no point in arguing with me, because I am smart and I am strong and I am right, and you are shy and you are fearful and you are wrong, and I win all the arguments, so don't even try. She was doing it now, Julia, mirroring Lydia's movement, asserting her superiority in this battle. Loggerheads.

It was what Tito'd said just before he left that gave Lydia courage. 'Lydia's double,' he'd called Julia. It had only dawned on her at that moment, for the first time: it worked both ways. She had thought all her life that people saw her as Julia's double, but of course Julia could be considered Lydia's double too. It was so obvious, and yet it had never occurred to her before. She could be the original and Julia the copy, just as easily as the other way around. It depended how you looked at it. It was a strangely stirring thought.

'Girls, girls,' said Frankie, 'you sound like five-year-olds fighting about their colouring pencils.'

'And you sound like a teacher,' said Lydia. 'Doesn't she, Julia?'

'Do keep out of it, Mum,' said Julia. 'This is girl stuff, no old ladies invited.'

'Yes, Mum,' said Lydia, 'and it's your and Dad's turn to wash up. How come he always disappears when it's your turn?'

'I'll get him,' said their mother, wearily.

'He likes me too,' said Julia, as their mother went. 'And he can't even get your name right. Anyway, I thought *you'd* fallen for Jonathan.'

'Jonathan?' said Lydia, as if recalling someone she'd known long ago, in a past life. She had pushed all thoughts of Jonathan firmly to the back of her mind, once Julia had made her realise he wasn't really interested in her. All the same, the place in her heart labelled 'Jonathan' was still tender. She didn't want to so much as press a fingertip to it. But she couldn't let Julia know that. 'I had one cup of coffee with Jonathan. It doesn't mean we're *married*. Anyway, who says I want your cast-offs?'

'I didn't cast him off,' said Julia. 'It was the other way around, remember?'

'It's twins' fate,' said Lydia. 'Falling for the same people. It probably goes on all the time, all over the world. We're probably typical of some observable phenomenon. It even happens in *The Curiosity Tree*, and that was yonks ago.'

'Hmm,' said Julia. 'OK. But look, Lydia, if you fancied Jonathan, instead of Tito, as I thought you did, then that'd be better, wouldn't it, because …'

'Because you don't want him?'

'I wouldn't have put it so bluntly,' said Julia, 'but yes, that's about it.'

Lydia laughed. 'Julia, life doesn't always work out the way you'd like it to.'

'Don't do it, Lydia, just don't go there. I hate it when you preach. I was only saying that it would be more convenient …'

'Well, I'm afraid I can't fall in love to suit your convenience, Jule.'

'No, but you fancied Jonathan last week.'

'So did you, Julia. So did you.'

The Curiosity Tree ③

'**D**id you ever see so many stars?' Sun´va asked. She reached up as if she meant to pluck one from the sky.

'There's always the same number of stars,' said Eva. 'You don't think they change?'

The girls had slipped out of their bed-chamber just before dawn. Sun´va was restless and wanted to go out, but she'd woken Eva as she dressed, and Eva had insisted on coming too.

'Of course they change!' said Sun´va. 'Sometimes you can see the Bear, sometimes the Hunter, nearly always the Plough.'

'Well, who moves them around, then?' asked Eva, screwing up her eyes. 'Is that the Plough?'

'The gods do, I suppose. Yes, that's the Plough.'

'Have you had enough fresh air yet?' Eva asked. 'Can we go back to bed now?'

'No,' said Sun´va. 'I need to run.'

'Run! You need to run! Did you not run enough today already?'

'I just need to run. I feel the urge to run to the beach.'

'Sun´va, what's going on?'

'I just feel the urge to run to the beach under the sta-aa-aa-ars.'

Sun´va's voice was high and excited, and she pulled the last word out so that it seemed to echo through itself. She was already starting to run, plucking Eva by the tunic to bring her along with her.

'We're going to the beach?' Eva panted as she hopped behind Sun´va from stepping stone to stepping stone.

'We are,' said Sun´va.

'But the Romans ...'

Ultan had decided that his best tactic was to pretend to assume that the Romans came in friendship, in order to buy time till his kinsmen and friends in the neighbouring countryside could be mustered to fight. And so he had let the Romans set up their camp by the cliffs, where now they waited, uneasily, to see how events turned out. The atmosphere was super-ficially friendly, though tension and suspicion hung in the air.

'Precisely,' said Sun´va. 'I want to get a proper look at them.'

'Sun´va! You're mad. They'll attack us if they see us.'

'They wouldn't dare,' said Sun´va. 'We are the chieftain's daughters. They've just made peace with Ultan. They won't want a war on their hands.'

'And just how are you going to explain to them that we are the chieftain's daughters? If we arrive at their camp in the middle of the night, they'll think we're common trollops.'

'Us? Look at us. Anyone can tell we're princesses!'

'Can they?'

'Of course they can,' said Sun´va. 'And anyway, it's not the middle of the night. It's nearly day. Come on!'

They had reached the lakeshore, and Sun´va had started to head off in the direction of the seashore.

'Sun´va, wait!' Eva couldn't keep up with her twin sister. She hadn't the same amount of running practice. 'So it's nearly day,' she went on, breathlessly. 'That means they'll be getting up and cooking their breakfast. They'll be all bleary-eyed and stubble-chinned, with bits of straw in their hair and smelly from sleeping in their clothes. What's wrong with you? You can't want to see them looking like that! Couldn't we at least wait till they've eaten their breakfast?'

'Hmmm,' said Sun´va, but she kept going. They were almost there.

'Sun´va,' Eva pleaded, 'I don't like this.'

'Well, go back to bed, then,' said Sun´va, and she flopped down on the cold, dawn-grey sand dunes that overlooked the beach.

Eva lay down on her stomach beside Sun´va. 'No point,' she said. 'You're right. It's nearly dawn.'

Together the girls looked out to sea, where the first pink glimmerings of daybreak streaked the horizon.

'Look!' hissed Sun´va, pointing to a figure crouching its way out of one of the low leather tents that were camped in the lee of the sand dunes.

The figure stood up now, with its back to the girls and its face to the sea, and stretched its arms. From where the girls lay staring, the figure was silhouetted dramatically against the dawn-pink sky.

'He looks like a hero, doesn't he?' breathed Sun´va.

'We-ell,' said Eva. 'I think he's just about to ... oh, don't look!'

The hero-silhouette lowered his arms and started fumbling with his clothing. He was clearly about to relieve himself.

Eva ducked quickly behind a sand dune and pulled

Sun´va with her.

'What's going on?' asked Sun´va, rolling onto her back.

'The Roman, he's … you know …' Eva slithered down beside her sister and put her hands over her eyes.

Sun´va clapped both hands over her mouth and laughed and laughed between her fingers.

'We shouldn't be watching, Sun´va. It's not right.'

'But we're not watching. We're facing in the opposite direction, for heaven's sake.'

'We can't stay here,' Eva said, lowering her hands from her eyes. 'Let's go home.'

'No,' said Sun´va. 'You can if you want to.'

'Sun´va, we can't stay here and watch people doing private things. It's not right.'

'Suppose we just lie here for a bit,' suggested Sun´va, 'until they've all got up and made themselves respectable, and then we can go to the top of the dunes again and take a peek. They'll be ready to receive visitors by then.'

'Oh, very well,' said Eva, suddenly too tired to argue any more, and she flung her arm out on the ground.

Sun´va rolled into the crook of her sister's arm like a sleepy kitten, and within minutes the two of them had fallen into a doze.

When Sun´va woke, there was only a wispy scrap of moon like a piece of discarded gauze on the sapphire sky, and the sun was up. The stars had long since faded from view. It was going to be another scorching day.

'Eva!' she whispered.

Eva's eyelids fluttered open. Immediately her hands sprang to her eyes to protect them from the sudden glare of morning.

'Ave!' said a light voice, and a shadow moved over the two girls, where they lay side by side.

Sun´va sat up and peered against the sunlight. It was one of the soldiers, a young one.

'Ave,' she tried, and nudged Eva to sit up also.

'Ave,' he said again. For heaven's sake, was he going to go on repeating these two syllables all morning?

'Yes,' she said. 'That's what I said. Ave.'

The young soldier laughed and shook his head. 'Ahh--vay,' he said with emphasis.

'What do you think he means, Eva?' Sun´va asked, keeping her eyes on the soldier. His hair was dark and curly and cropped tight against his head. His eyes were like two dark stones from the bottom of a stream, somewhere between grey and brown and with a sort of a silvery gleam to them, as if little silvery fishes darted through them. 'And by all the gods,' she added, 'isn't he handsome!'

'You're not pronouncing it right,' said Eva.

'Ave,' said Sun´va again, and the young soldier laughed.

'Sun´va,' she said then, pointing to herself. 'And Eva.' She pointed to Eva.

The boy shook his head.

'Sun´va,' she said patiently. 'Suh-neh-veh. Sun´va.'

'Sunn-e-va?'

'Yes. And Eva. Eee-fa.'

'Eefa.'

'He can pronounce my name better than yours,' said Eva smugly.

'You have a very common name,' said Sun´va. 'Mine is

special. It takes getting used to.'

'Flavius,' the boy-soldier said then, pointing to himself. 'Fla-vee-ous.'

'Fllya-vius?' Sun´va attempted.

'Fla-vius.'

'Fill-a-vius,' Sun´va tried.

'Flavius,' said Eva simply.

Flavius nodded vigorously. Sun´va glared at her.

'Well, it's easy,' said Eva. 'Flavius.'

'Duo?' said Flavius, looking from one girl to the other and holding up two fingers.

'What does that mean?' Sun´va asked, exasperated.

'Duo,' said Eva, nodding at Flavius. 'Two, it means two, Sun´va. He means, there are two of us.'

'Well of course there are two of us,' said Sun´va grumpily.

'No, silly, he means we're twins.'

'Well, well,' said Sun´va, 'very observant of him, I must say.'

'I thought you liked him.'

'I do. I just don't think he's got much to say for himself.'

'He's doing his best,' said Eva tolerantly. 'People always want to talk about how alike we are. That's all he means.'

'We're only physically alike,' Sun´va said to Flavius, who shrugged his shoulders.

'Fortunately,' Eva added. 'Don't worry, he hasn't a clue what we're saying. You're right, though, he is handsome.'

'I saw him first,' shouted Sun´va. 'I spoke to him first,

I was the one who wanted to come here. He's mine!'

'But he's a foreigner,' said Eva. 'You can't get mixed up with a foreigner, an enemy. And anyway, you are promised to Cormac, son of the king of Meath.'

'That's only a formality. Ultan would never make me marry anyone I didn't want to, even if it were the most favourable marriage contract in the world. Anyway, who mentioned marriage? I just like the look of this Roman, that's all. I'm not planning on marrying anyone.'

'Still,' said Eva unhappily, 'you cannot fall in love with a Roman.'

'Love? Who said anything about love?'

'Love?' said Flavius.

'No!' shouted the twins together and shook their heads vehemently.

'No love?' said Flavius.

'Here, talk about something else, quick, Eva,' said Sun´va. 'We can't have him talking like that. If Ultan heard him!'

Eva drew her hands together, one over the other, palm down and then made a sharp movement with each hand in a different direction. She scissored her hands together again and repeated the movement. And she did it a third time, and shook her head. 'No!' she said.

Flavius nodded. 'Duo,' he said again.

'Yes, duo,' said Eva. 'That's right. Numbers are fine.'

'Venite!' said Flavius suddenly. He turned towards the beach and beckoned to them with his arm. 'Venite.'

'I think he wants us to go down to the camp with him,' said Sun´va. 'Hey!'

'We can't.'

'Venite!' repeated Flavius.

'We can,' said Sun´va and grasped Eva by the elbow. 'Of course we can.'

CHAPTER 8

Thou knowest my daughter's of a pretty age
Romeo & Juliet Act 1, Sc iii

Julia had a good view from her attic room, not just out over the sea, but also of next-door's garden. There was a solitary, un-pruned apple tree there, and a tattered old hammock swung out of it, left behind by the family who used to live in the house. That afternoon, Julia had noticed that someone was bundled in the hammock, and she had a hunch that it might be Tito. Lydia'd gone shopping for a new pair of jeans, so the coast was clear.

Julia appeared suddenly in the kitchen, much to Frankie's surprise, and said she thought the house needed brightening up.

'I know,' she volunteered, 'I'll cut some flowers ... eh ... roses?' She hoped there were roses in the garden. She couldn't remember for sure. She didn't think she'd been in the garden for months.

'OK,' said Frankie, mystified, and told her where the secateurs were.

The rose-cutting gave Julia the perfect excuse to be in the garden, and the opportunity to call a greeting to Tito over the wall. He tumbled out of his hammock, right on cue, and came to talk to her.

'Hello,' she said again, fiddling with the plastic handles of the secateurs, which stuck out of her pocket, and idly sniffing the bunch of roses she'd cut, searching desperately for something to say. She hadn't thought this far ahead.

'Hello,' he said, with a slow, slightly puzzled smile.

'What do your people think of arranged marriages?' she blurted out suddenly. She clapped her hand over her mouth as soon as she'd said it. What a stupid, patronising question! She, of course, did not approve of arranged marriages, but asking this strange boy about such a thing was absurd, rude, possibly even racist. She'd crossed a line she shouldn't have, she knew it, not with a person she hardly knew. She couldn't take the wretched question back now, though, however much she wished she hadn't asked it.

'Arranged marriages?' said Tito warily. He looked at her gravely, appearing to take the question seriously. Maybe it wasn't so bad. Perhaps it was a clever question after all. It was the sort of thing people – reporters, anthropologists – asked in television documentaries.

Thoughts raced through her mind, as she waited to see what he would say. You can't get mixed up with a foreigner, Eva'd said to Sun'va. Of course, that was two thousand years ago. Things were different. And yet Dad … But of course, she couldn't ask Tito what he thought of *that*. That'd be even worse than asking about arranged marriages.

'Only … eh, it's in this book I've been reading,' she added, galloping, hoping to explain her way out of it, 'so I just wondered.'

Tito wondered whether this bright-haired Irish girl with a bunch of flowers in her hand was Julia or Lydia, but he didn't like to ask, so he avoided using her name.

'Who said anything to you about arranged marriages?' he asked, looking into her strangely light grey-green eyes.

He'd met white people before, lots of them, especially since coming here, but they'd mostly been lank-haired, pasty-skinned, dull-eyed. He'd never before seen anyone who looked like these Irish girls, with their moss-green, rock-grey eyes and their hair, all twisted and flimsy, of a colour he couldn't describe, somewhere between yellow and pink, and with tiny sprinklings, like flattened grains of brown sugar, on their soft, pale, pink-flushed skin. They looked to him fragile, almost transparent, as if they might blow away on the wind at any moment.

'Nobody,' said Julia, who was in no danger at all of blowing away. He sounded suspicious. Just what she didn't want. 'It's only that, like I say, this book I'm reading … We had arranged marriages in Ireland.' She noted the surprised look on his face; well, at least surprise was better than suspicion. 'A long time ago,' she jabbered on. 'I mean, this book is set in *ancient* times, but of course it's not that long since marriages were arranged. Nowadays, people choose, of course, but even, oh, a hundred years ago …' She was blathering. She knew it. She stopped suddenly.

There was a silence for a while. At last Tito spoke. 'In my country,' he began carefully, 'marriages are often arranged.'

'Yes?' said Julia, relaxing now that he seemed prepared to talk about it. She might as well see it through, now that she'd gone this far. 'And?'

'And what?'

'And do they work?'

'Work?' said Tito. He'd only ever heard this sort of expression applied to something like a washing machine. He'd never thought of a human sort of arrangement like marriage 'working'. It was just something that was organised, and that happened, and then life went on in the usual way, with just a shift in generations.

'Yes,' said Julia, to whom it was not only a sensible question, but really the only question worth asking about marriage. 'Are they happy?'

'Happy?' said Tito. 'Who? Are who happy?'

'The people who get married, of course,' said Julia.

Tito shrugged. 'Happy?' Again, he'd never heard this word applied in the way Julia was using it. In his view, happiness was a matter of temperament or maybe luck. That seemed so obvious to him that the question made no sense. He didn't see what it could possibly have to do with marriage. 'They have children,' he ventured.

'Yes?' said Julia, encouragingly.

'Many children,' said Tito, encouraged.

'Not too many, I hope,' said Julia.

'Eh, no,' said Tito, sensing that this was the right thing to say.

He hesitated for a moment. He'd told nobody, apart from Catherine, of course, about his sister, but Catherine was different. He'd hugged his story to himself, only breaking off tiny bits of it from time to time for the consumption of the authorities, when it was really necessary. In his view, his past, his life in his own country – all that was private, it had to do with him and his family, not with people in offices filling out forms. But sometimes it got tiring, hugging your story to yourself, especially when it was such a heavy story to have to carry around all the time, like a dead child in your arms, dragging out of you everywhere you went. He was weary of it.

And now here was this girl, this fragile-looking creature, standing there in this nice, safe, Dublin back garden, her hands full of roses, beautiful red and yellow roses, with the rumble of a bus going by on the main road to the front of the house and the cry of a seagull swooping overhead. And she'd asked. She'd asked about arranged marriages. She must be interested, though he couldn't work out why. Maybe, he thought, maybe this was someone he could tell the story to, or some of it, unburden himself at least for a little while, get a rest from lugging it around all the time.

Once he started, it all began to come tumbling out, word after word, almost without his having to think about what he was saying.

'My sister, Nkemi, see, she was twelve. A very old man, he wanted to marry her. My uncle, he thought this was a good idea, since he would get a good piece of field when they married.'

'Oh no!' said Julia, horrified. 'Your uncle wanted to *sell* her? For land?'

'*No!*' Tito clammed up as suddenly as he had started to pour his story out. It had been a mistake to try. She wouldn't understand. She took a different view. They were poles apart. This was a private story, not for telling over a garden wall to the first person who asked him about it. But now he'd made her misunderstand, made her think his uncle was a greedy man. He couldn't just leave it like that.

'Well, what then?' she asked.

Tito shook his head. He couldn't find the words to continue.

'Sorry,' said Julia.

There now, she'd opened up something he didn't want to talk about. She'd distressed him, she could see. Once again, she wished she'd never started this conversation. It was going to places she hadn't expected and didn't want to visit.

Tito sighed. How could he make her understand, this fresh-faced Irish girl with her bunch of sweet roses and her sense of humour bubbling and winking – he could practically see it – under her cautious, pink-lipped smile? What could he tell her that would make her understand that sharp, hot country that he came from, with its blazing colours and its flaming conflicts? It was like trying to explain the stars to a person who lived underground. There was no point. He shook his head again.

'But then,' he concluded, 'she died, so it didn't happen.'

'She *died?*' Julia's shock came through in her voice. 'But I thought you said she was only twelve.'

Tito swallowed. He had to go on. It wasn't fair to Julia to stop now. And it wasn't fair to Nkemi.

'It was … well, it was on a journey, a hard journey. We walked for miles.'

'A journey on foot?'

'Not only. We stole bicycles. We rode them till they fell apart. We went by train, in the toilet, because we didn't have a ticket. We went inside a container vehicle, in between the crates. Always cramped places. And hot. I thought we would suffocate before we would make it.'

He meant the journey here, she realised. Nkemi had died on the way to Ireland. Julia had read about that sort of thing. Awful stories about people in containers, dead on arrival.

'But what happened to Nkemi? Did she … oh, Tito, she didn't suffocate?'

She clenched the roses too tightly and tears sprang in her

eyes as a thorn stabbed her finger. She transferred the roses to the other hand and regarded the bead of blood that started to swell on the pad of her finger. She stuck it in her mouth, and the metallic taste of blood crept over her tongue.

Tito drew his hand down over his face, like a blind closing. Julia held her breath. Had she said the wrong thing again? But then, after a few moments, Tito spoke again.

'No,' he said. 'She stepped on a nail.'

'A nail? She stepped on a nail?'

'She liked to run barefoot.'

'But … stepping on a nail – does that kill you?'

'It was on a ship, down in the hold. It smells of grease and rancid fish and tarry ropes, horrible, and it's hot, and the engine thumps all the time, it gets into your body, like a second heart. She was running around among the cargo. It got infected, her foot. Blood poisoning. I was seasick, too sick to bother about a child with a sore foot. The poison, it was in all her body. I got a doctor, when I knew it was serious, but it was too late.' He shrugged sadly and stopped talking.

Julia could hear her own heartbeat in her ears.

'She was so young,' Tito went on after a while, his voice lightening, a small smile starting out of the sadness of his face. It was as if he had forgotten about Julia. He wasn't looking at her. He seemed to be talking to himself. 'She didn't know how dangerous it was. She thought it was like being runaways in a story.'

Julia stared, willing him to go on, because she knew she couldn't say anything, she just couldn't open her mouth.

He turned right away for a moment, looking into the garden on his own side of the wall. Apart from the elderly apple tree Tito'd been lying under, nothing grew there, only tufty grass and a lot of dandelion leaves. In spring it was paved with dandelion gold, but at this time of year even the dandelion clocks were over and the garden looked like a huge, patchy and rather weary salad. A small breeze rustled the branches of the tree and an undersize apple plopped onto the yellowing grass. Tito sighed and then turned back to Julia.

He was in another place now, and his face was full of smiling. He looked right at her and spoke directly to her. 'She laughed. She danced under the stars. She sang to me when I was so hungry that I couldn't sleep.'

Julia smiled too, relieved at this change in his mood.

'But then …' A cloud descended over his features again. 'I tried to be a good brother, to save her from danger. But I couldn't. I failed.'

'Oh, Tito,' said Julia, 'I am so sorry!'

Tito looked at her strangely. 'It is not your fault.'

'I mean,' said Julia, 'I mean I am sad for you. And sorry I made you talk about it. I didn't mean to make you remember.'

'No, no,' said Tito. 'I *like* to remember Nkemi. She is a funny girl. Always laughing, joking. She smelt of toffee.

She wore a pink dress. She loved to play. She was only a child.'

'Oh dear,' said Julia. 'Poor Tito.'

Tito looked surprised again. 'No,' he said, '*I* am Tito. My sister's name is Nkemi. Poor Nkemi, you mean, poor Nkemi.'

'Yes,' said Julia. 'That too. Poor Nkemi. Here, have these.' She thrust the roses at him. 'Careful,' she said, 'they're thorny. But they smell fantastic. Put them in water.'

'Why?'

'Flowers need water.'

'No,' said Tito, 'I mean, why do you give them to me, these roses?'

'Oh!' said Julia. It had been an impulse. She'd wanted to do something for him, give him something, when she'd heard about his sister. 'It's what we do when people die. Give flowers.'

'Ah,' said Tito. 'They're for Nkemi? Flowers for Nkemi.'

'Yes, yes,' said Julia desperately, embarrassed now by her own gesture, wishing she could disappear. But she couldn't – that would be rude, and unkind. 'Flowers for Nkemi,' she added. Oddly, it sounded OK when she repeated his words. Her embarrassment started to dissolve.

'Thank you,' Tito said formally, simply, bowing slightly over the bunch of flowers.

'You're welcome,' Julia gasped. 'Eh … bye now, I have to go.'

She turned then and fled into the house, because she knew if she spoke another word, she would cry and cry and cry, and she thought she might never be able to stop.

The Curiosity Tree 4

Within a day of the landing of the Romans, Ultan had summoned every kinsman he had for miles around and everyone of his wife's kin too and his son-in-law's people, and everyone who owed him debts of money, or kind, and everyone who owed him homage. It amounted to hundreds of warriors, all come, ostensibly, to the feast of Lunasa, but all armed and ready to do battle. When he had gathered sufficient fighting men to intimidate the Romans for real this time, Ultan led them, bristling with weapons, down to the Roman camp on the beach.

The next part of Ultan's plan was about to unfold. The feast of Lunasa was upon them, and he did not want to ruin the feasting with war-making, and so he had planned to invite the Romans to join the Irish for the feast, put them at their ease, get them intoxicated even. And once dawn came and the feast was over, then it would be soon enough to do battle with these invaders and rout them from the soil of Ireland.

Using creative sign language, Ultan managed to convey the message to Tullius, the Roman leader, that he was inviting the men of Rome to join the Irish at their feast of Lunasa.

Tullius was wary. His company had been sent here on a reconnaissance mission, and he'd hoped to avoid conflict with the natives. He'd fought in enough campaigns, and he was looking forward to retiring. He had a plan to buy a small vineyard and settle to country life. The last thing he wanted was to do battle – but he would if he had to.

He had been taken aback when Ultan had welcomed him and his troops ashore. He knew all about the legendary ferocity of the Celts, and once he realised that their boats had been spotted, he'd been prepared to have to fight his way to shore. But now they were apparently inviting them to some sort of banquet. What was going on? His instinct was not to trust the Celts, but at the same time, he didn't feel right about going to war with a people who had shown nothing but courtesy to him and his men. Accepting this invitation would only draw him further into these people's debt – and yet, what choice did he have? For if he refused, the Irish would be justified in being insulted and might very well want to fight right now. Tullius' men were not the finest army Rome had to offer – they were just a reconnaissance posse after all – so, throwing caution to the winds, and with a series of bows and smiles, he accepted Ultan's invitation. He posted a discreet guard around the camp, to be on the safe side, and led the remainder of his men to the area of the beach indicated for them, where they sat and joined the festivities.

The celebrations began, at the Irish end of the beach, with the lighting of fires and the ritual sacrifice of birds and animals to Lu, god of harvest and god of war. Tullius had heard that sometimes the Celts sacrificed human beings. He was relieved that it was only a pair of bullocks and some fowl that were put to death. Manus the druid observed the entrails of the sacrificed beasts and proclaimed good fortune for the people for another year and a harvest next year to equal this one. Then the meat was divided among the people, and corn and milk were left, with a portion of meat, for the god.

'That means more sunshine,' said Sun´va, when she heard Manus's words. She threw her hair over her shoulder and lifted her face to what was left of the sun as it slid quietly over the bogland to the west.

'The sun doesn't shine specially for you to enjoy, you know,' said Eva.

'I know that. The sun-god shines to kiss Macha, the earth-god, so that she produces grass and crops and berries and fruits, and so long as the people observe the rituals, he shines and shines all summer long to ripen the corn and swell the fruits. But we may as well enjoy it too. When we soak up its heat, it doesn't mean there is any less for the crops. The sun's goodness is infinite!'

Manus heard her and turned to see who spoke.

'Sun´va daughter of Ultan,' he said, 'you understand the ways of heaven.'

'Oh!' said Sun´va, taken aback that she had been overheard, but she stood up and bowed deeply to Manus. 'Thank you, O Wise One!' she murmured. 'Do you hear that?' she said, nudging Eva as she sat down again. 'I understand the ways of heaven!'

Ultan left his place at the head of the feasting and brought a young man to Sun´va's side. The young man was dark-browed and had a slightly jutting forehead, which cast a shadow over his face. But his jaw was firm and his mouth wide, giving him a generous, open look, and under his fierce brow, his eyes were blue as flowers. Sun´va shot him a small, shy smile, and looked enquiringly at her father.

'Sun´va daughter of Ultan,' said Ultan, formally, 'I present to you Cormac son of Cuan, king of Meath.'

'Oh!' said Sun´va, surprised. So this was Cormac son of Cuan, to whom she had been betrothed since they were children. If they liked each other, now that they were of an age to marry, then both their fathers would be pleased to have a bond of marriage and kinship between their two clans. Sun´va could read that hope in Ultan's eyes as he pushed Cormac forward.

He was handsome enough, to be sure, this Cormac, and he looked strong and brave. Sun´va bowed to Cormac and smiled at Ultan. She might consider marrying him, her smile seemed to say. He might do. If she were to marry at all, that was, maybe some day, in the far distant future, when she had fully grown out of climbing trees and speeding through the forest.

But when the dancing started, it was Flavius, the boy-soldier she'd met the previous morning at the beach, that Sun´va went to find. She wandered down to the part of the beach where the Romans sat feasting, slipping in and out between the enemy ranks under cover of the late dusk, and found him, sitting with Tullius, the Roman leader. Tullius had a large piece of meat in his hands, and grease dripped from his chin. He had decided after all to enjoy the feast. There was no point in meeting trouble before it started.

'The Celts are a fine race,' he was saying to Flavius, whom he had known at home in Rome since Flavius was a baby. 'They know how to lay on a feast. I like a tribe who can slaughter a beast and crack open the ale barrels.'

'Fill-avius,' Sun´va called. 'Come and join the dance!'

Flavius turned, at the sound of her voice, a flame racing in his cheeks.

'Dance?' he said, copying the sound Sun´va made. '*Rince.*'

'Yes!' said Sun´va, lifting the hem of her best linen tunic over her ankles and dancing on the sands to show him what the word meant. '*Rince*! We dance at the feast of Lunasa. Dance, Fill-avius. *Rince*!'

Flavius shook his head. He didn't think his old friend and mentor and now his commander, Tullius, would approve of him going to the dancing with the daughter of the enemy, even if they were all pretending to be friends. And anyway, dancing didn't come naturally to him. He didn't want to make a fool of himself in front of this girl. '*Romani no rince!*' he muttered.

'Romans don't dance?' Sun´va laughed. He couldn't be serious. She looked to Tullius.

'*Romani no rince,*' confirmed Tullius, wiping his mouth with the back of his hand. 'No *rince* in Rome.'

'But you're not in Rome!' exclaimed Sun´va, pulling at Flavius' sleeve to drag him to where the dancers were shuffling into place on the hard-packed sand close to the tideline. 'Come on!'

'*Romani – no – rince!*' said Flavius through gritted teeth, trapped now in his own confusion. He refused to budge, though he longed to snatch Sun´va into his arms and fly with her to where the dancing was happening. But he couldn't. He couldn't lift his Roman feet and follow her. Everything about his upbringing and what he considered proper anchored him to the spot.

Sun´va was startled by the fierceness of his opposition to her.

'Very well,' she said, dropping his sleeve. 'But in this country, dancing is important. We dance to placate the gods. I hope you haven't offended Lu, and that your surly behaviour doesn't affect the crops next year, because if it has, my father will not be pleased with you.'

Flavius had no idea what she was saying, but he could see that she was insulted. He caught her wrist in his hand as if to plead with her to understand, but she snatched her hand away as if his was on fire and flounced off to join the other young people of her tribe.

Sun´va, her eyes smarting with shame and anger, went pushing and shouldering her way through the crowds at her own end of the beach, looking for Cormac now. He'd gone off gaming, somebody told her.

Sun´va knew it was her own fault that Cormac had disappeared. She'd given him the slip when the dancing started, and now that she'd been rejected by Flavius, she could hardly expect Cormac to be waiting for her. But she was cross with him all the same. She strode off angrily to climb her curiosity tree. From there, she might be able to spy out Cormac among the crowd, in the starlight. It would be easier than trying to find him in the mass of people on the beach.

As soon as she raised her foot to climb the tree, Sun´va realised she couldn't do it in her fancy long feasting tunic. So she yanked the annoying garment over her head, easing it over the golden torc she wore around her neck, and threw it in a soft pile of folds on the ground. Freed from her awkward clothing, she shinned up the tree easily in her shift, shivering slightly in the night air, though it wasn't really cold.

From the branches of her tree, Sun´va couldn't spot Cormac, but she saw Flavius where she'd left him, kicking angrily in the sand and talking with awkward, elbowy gesticulations to Tullius. What could those two be arguing about? she wondered. She hoped Tullius was giving him a good talking-to about how to treat a lady. This wasn't a word Sun´va often applied to herself, but from time to time it was useful to remember that she was, after all, the daughter of the chieftain. She tossed her head in her perch in the tree as if to shake Flavius off.

As Sun´va flounced away from him, Flavius spun around on the sand and kicked a length of dried-out bladderwrack with his toe.

'Damn,' he muttered.

Tullius laughed.

'Don't laugh,' said Flavius.

'But why are you so irritable, boy? You are quite right: Romans don't dance. It's bad form, where we come from. She has to accept that.'

'Cornelia …' muttered Flavius.

Cornelia was Flavius' betrothed, at home in Rome. They'd been promised to one another since childhood, and they'd planned their wedding for the autumn, when Flavius returned from his tour of duty in Britain. Cornelia was a quiet girl, from a good family, not rich but hardworking, and Flavius' mother was happy to think of her son with such a suitable wife. Flavius was inclined to be hot-headed, his mother said, and a girl like Cornelia would soothe him into better moods. She wouldn't argue with him when he was angry or try to tell him what to do, and that, in his mother's view, was just what Flavius needed, a willing, compliant wife who would rule her household by stealth rather than through confrontation.

'Ah,' said Tullius, and he nodded sympathetically. 'Torn between two attractive young women. Dear me, what it is to be young.'

Flavius looked away, out to where the Roman ships lay beached. They were his nearest connection to his dark-eyed Cornelia. But the ships were ghosts in the eerie light of the summer night, too far from the feasting to be lit by the shifting firelight, spectral outlines against the starlit water.

'If I were you,' Tullius was saying, waving a beaker of ale, 'I'd go after that young lady and apologise. I'd dance till dawn, if I were you.'

Flavius looked at Tullius. He'd changed his tune.

'You're drunk,' Flavius said, matter-of-factly.

'Not at all, my boy. It won't do the least harm to find that girl now, and Cornelia will still be there when you get home.'

Flavius sighed. The logic of the adult world still amazed him. If Tullius couldn't see what was wrong with that line of reasoning, then maybe he shouldn't be able to see it either. Maybe he was stuck in some flawed, childhood way of thinking, going by the heart instead of the head. But to his way of looking at it, he couldn't do this thing that he wanted to do and still go to Cornelia when he got home. According to Flavius' thinking, he had to choose, whereas Tullius seemed to think he could have it both ways.

'And don't sigh about it,' Tullius said. 'No need to make such heavy weather of it. Enjoy yourself, for the sake of the gods. And anyway, if you become friendly with the daughter of the chieftain, that can only be good for relations between our two nations. I'd prefer you to go to the dancing with that young Celtic noblewoman than for us all to have to fight this Celtic army.'

Flavius kicked the bladderwrack some more.

'Well, maybe I will try to find her, so,' he said wearily, though he only half-wanted to. And yet the half that did want to find her was pulling more strongly than the half of him that preferred to hang back.

'That's the way!'

Flavius' mind was in turmoil, as it had been since he had met Sun´va on the dunes that first morning. She had shone in the early sun, and tonight, in the firelight, she seemed to sparkle. He had never seen such golden hair before. And those greeny cats' eyes of hers! Tullius was right. It could do the Roman position no harm if they were to get on friendly terms with the natives. It would be a patriotic act after all to go and find Sun´va.

'Go,' said Tullius. 'For the sake of the Empire, go and find that girl. It's your duty as a Roman.'

'My duty!'

Tullius smiled. 'Yes. In fact, I command you to go to the dancing with her.'

Flavius laughed. 'Well, if you insist ...' He girded his short sword around him and picked up his shield. Then he looked at the shield and decided against it. Too awkward, and anyway, it made him look suspicious. He threw it on the ground. It made a dull thud as it landed. Tullius leapt backwards, as if he thought the shield was going to land on his toes.

'*Salve*,' said Tullius with mock solemnity. He raised his arm in valediction. Flavius waved and turned away.

He didn't go straight to the dancing, though. Instead, he scrambled over the dunes and headed towards the edge of the forest. He didn't know how far he would get into the forest before it became too dark to see, but he'd try anyway

From her position in the curiosity tree, Sun´va had not been able to catch sight of Cormac. Instead, she watched Flavius wave at Tullius and make off across the beach. He was coming towards her. Yes, yes, he was coming to find her! She smiled with satisfaction. He'd changed his mind. But how could he know about the curiosity tree? Had he seen her making off in the direction of the woods? Had he been watching, following her path with his eyes all along, when she thought he'd been hanging his head in confusion?

She watched as Flavius came closer and closer. Yes, he was definitely coming towards her. He must be sorry. Oh well, it was probably only shyness. Foreigners were different. They didn't understand our ways. How could they? They had different customs in Rome, no doubt. She decided to forgive him. As soon as he reached her tree, she thought, she'd slither down the trunk, into his arms and ... well, then, anything could happen.

When he reached the oak tree at the edge of the woods, Flavius stopped and leaned against its trunk for a moment to look back at the beach. Shadows and flame-red licks of light leapt at each other over the sands, and the sounds of laughter and chatter came to him over the constant hiss and soft roar of the sea.

Sun´va, crouched in the tree, was just about to lower her hand and stroke the curls of his head. She imagined how white and ghostly her arm would look in the dark. But then she remembered that she'd taken off her tunic. She couldn't very well slither down the tree in her shift! She'd have to stay put and work out a way to get hold of her tunic.

But while she was puzzling over this problem, Flavius moved away, stepping carefully into the edge of the woods. What could he be at? Clearly he didn't know Sun´va was there in the tree above him after all. But then, what could he be up to? She stayed as still as she could manage on her branch, and breathed as softly as she could, and watched.

Even craning her neck, though, she couldn't see much, now that he had disappeared into the undergrowth, but she could hear him scuffling in the brush. What on earth ...?

Flavius pressed on, into the woods. It was getting darker already, here where the firelight couldn't reach, but there was plenty of starlight and the moon was now climbing the sky, so with a little effort he could make out where he was going. He didn't need to go very far into the wood before he found what he was looking for – a tangle of bushy under-growth putting out languorous, scented arms into the night air. He hunkered down and started pulling, and within minutes he had an armful of greenery.

Sun´va watched, puzzled, as he emerged from the woods at a semi-run, trailing greenery and flowers, like some demented dryad, racing towards the firelit dunes.

Flavius sat down on the night-chilled sands, and quickly started to plait a garland from the green stuff he had gath-ered. His mother worked occasionally in a Roman florist's shop, and as a child he had learnt the skill of plaiting gar-lands for the feasts that went on in the houses of the rich. No one in Rome would dream of giving a feast without pro-viding garlands for all their guests, and if he were going to break the Roman taboo on dancing, he would at least observe the Roman custom of placing a garland on his beloved's head.

No, that's not right, he told himself, as he severed a twin-ing woodbine stem with his teeth. Sun´va is not my beloved. She is just a pretty girl who wants me to dance. That is all.

He held the garland out to inspect it. It didn't have the professional look that his mother's garlands had. This loose Irish green stuff was harder to manage than the small, sweet flowers and neat, narrow leaves of the jasmine that grew on the Latinate hills. It would do, though. It was charming, even, in a wild sort of way. And it smelt delicious. He buried his nose in the deep rosy heads of summer honeysuckle, flowers that opened thin red lips to reveal creamy-yellow insides and release a heady perfume.

CHAPTER 9

Young men's love, then, lies
Not truly in their hearts, but in their eyes
Romeo & Juliet Act 2, Sc iii

They hardly ever used the local shop, because it was expensive, but as Frankie said, you didn't think of a thing like cornflour when you were doing the weekly grocery shopping. They didn't think of it in the convenience store either, apparently, because Lydia couldn't find it. She was hunkered down, looking on the lowest shelf, where they kept the less-bought items, like pearl barley and gelatine, when she heard a voice from very far above her.

'Hello,' said Tito from a height.

His face was made convex by the odd perspective. She stood up in a hurry, anxious to face him at a more reasonable angle, and saw stars for a moment. She put out a hand to steady herself and Tito caught her by the wrist.

'You OK?' he asked.

'Yes,' she gasped, looking at the dark bands his fingers made across her forearm. 'Just a rush of blood to the head.'

'Oh?' he said in alarm. 'Sounds bad!'

'It's nothing,' she said. She was fully back to herself now. 'Sorry if I gave you a scare. Did you think it was serious?'

She examined his face. It was an open, pleasant face, but she surprised herself by noting that he was not as handsome as Jonathan after all. She thought she'd stopped thinking about Jonathan, but clearly she hadn't. She shook her head slightly, as if to shake him out of it. Ever since the morning she'd heard the joyous voice of a living musician coming from Julia's sound system, she knew it was definitely, officially over – Julia was no longer in mourning for Jonathan. But now that Julia had released him back into general circulation, so to speak, Lydia'd lost interest in him, or thought she had. She couldn't be sure. Tito eclipsed everything at the moment, she'd thought. Yet now that she stood facing him, making small talk, images of Jonathan walked through her mind, even though she hadn't caught so much as a glimpse of him for days, not in the CD shop, where she'd been several times, 'just looking', nor near the flash cappuccino bar either, down at the harbour.

'It sounds like a brain haemorrhage,' Tito said, dropping her arm, 'a rush of blood in the head.' His features were puckered with anxiety.

Lydia laughed. 'No, no, it's just an expression. I stood up too fast, that's all. How … eh, how are things? How are you all settling in?' What a stupid question! She sounded like her mother. Why couldn't she think of something sparkling to say? Julia probably would. She picked a thread off the sleeve of her shirt, for an excuse to look away for a moment from Tito's gaze.

Tito ignored the question. 'I put the roses in water,' he said instead. 'You know, the flowers for Nkemi.'

'N-o,' said Lydia. 'Is that a film? Or a song? "Flowers for N–", for who?'

'Nkemi,' said Tito. And then he realised. 'Oh sorry, you must be the wrong twin,' he said. 'Which one are you?'

'Lydia,' said Lydia coolly. She didn't like being called 'the wrong twin'. There wasn't anything wrong with her.

'So it must have been Julia who gave me the roses. I'm sorry.'

'Julia gave you *roses*?'

'Yes,' said Tito, 'red ones and yellow ones. Beautiful. They smell so flagrant.'

'Fragrant,' said Lydia, with a small smile, in spite of her irritation at Julia. His mistake was oddly appropriate.

'Fragrant,' Tito repeated. 'Yes, that's what I mean. What were you looking for, when you were sitting on the floor?'

'Cornflour. My mother wants it for some sort of sauce she's making.'

'Is this it?' he asked, stretching out his long, slim hand and taking a box from a high shelf, way above Lydia's reach.

'Oh, thank you,' she said.

'Well,' he said, 'I must be … em, say thank you to Julia for me, will you, please? For the roses. Goodbye, Libby.'

'Lydia,' said Lydia.

'Yes,' said Tito. 'Sorry. Libya, of course.'

Lydia sighed softly to herself and went to the cash desk to pay for the cornflour. Julia – how did she manage it? Roses! *Roses*!

CHAPTER 10

Here comes your father; tell him so yourself,
And see how he will take it at your hands
Romeo & Juliet Act 3, Sc v

'Let's have a party,' Lydia suggested. 'To cheer us up. To make up to ourselves for having had such a dreary summer.'

The 'dreary summer' was code for the Jonathan business.

'That's a brilliant idea. We can invite Tito.'

'Among others,' said Lydia, careful not to be over-enthusiastic.

'I thought you liked Tito,' said Julia.

'I do,' said Lydia. 'And speaking of him,' she went on, deliberately, 'I hear you have been giving him flowers.'

'Flowers? Oh, you mean the roses, yes. Who told you?'

'He did.'

'You've been talking to Tito!' Julia was astounded at this departure from usual practice on Lydia's part. 'You never told me.'

'You never told *me* about the roses,' countered Lydia.

'Oh, but that …,' explained Julia, 'no, it's not what you think. They were for his sister.'

Lydia raised an eyebrow. 'Really? He's got a sister?'

'No,' said Julia. 'I mean, she … oh, it's a long story. But, about this party. It … it could be an unbirthday party.'

'The roses, Julia. Tell me about the roses, the sister.'

'No,' said Julia firmly, suddenly aware of how much she wanted to keep Tito's story for herself. 'I want to talk about the unbirthday party instead. Because it's *not* our birthday, see? And you have to have a theme for parties, so "un" can be the theme.'

Lydia allowed herself to be deflected, and the twins threw themselves into the preparations for the unbirthday party. Their friends were starting to trickle back to town from far-flung places, and this party could be the highpoint of the last weeks before term started again. Parties, as Julia said to Lydia, were full of possibilities. You never knew your luck, she said.

She concocted an invitation on the computer:

You are invited to Julia and Lydia's unbirthday party
Unpresents unwelcome!
Undress code: wild!
Unhamburgers and unchips served at 10pm

'What are unpresents?' asked Lydia. 'Empty parcels?'

'Whatever,' said Julia, with a touch of wildness in her voice. 'They can interpret it any way they like.'

'Well, I won't even ask about the undress code, but what are unhamburgers and unchips?'

'The opposite of hamburgers and chips. In other

words, something truly delicious and possibly vegetarian,' said Julia, 'obviously.'

'Well, while you are being so obvious, you might mention the date and the address on your invitation, and there is the little matter of Mum and Dad.'

In the event, Frankie and Ray put up no resistance.

'As you cannot fail to have noticed,' said Ray, with a smirk, 'we are quite the most co-operative parents in town.'

'Absolutely,' said Julia happily. 'Possibly in the world. I've always said so.'

'Hmm,' said Ray, 'you certainly have not.'

All the same, to the girls' delight, he offered to pay for the food.

'Thank you,' said Julia, hugging her father, 'my little Ray of sunshine!'

'But there is just one thing,' Ray said.

Julia froze. He was going to say they couldn't invite anyone from next door. She knew it. She just *knew*. There'd been an uneasy truce between herself and her father in recent days about the asylum seekers, but now it was all going to flare up again.

'Don't say it, Dad!' she hissed.

'But I must,' he said.

'Please, Dad, don't spoil it,' she pleaded.

'No, Julia, that's not fair. I have to insist …'

'Da-a-ad!'

'No alcohol,' said Ray firmly, 'because you're under-age and I am not taking responsibility for other people's children drinking, whatever about my own, and anyway, there is nothing worse than drunken ...'

'Oh Dad! Is that all!' Julia didn't drink anyway. 'No booze, no problem.'

'*And* ... ' Frankie chimed in.

'What now?' said Julia. 'Have *you* got a condition as well?'

'Yes,' said Frankie.

'Well,' said Julia, her hands to her head, 'out with it. Quick! I can't stand the tension.'

'That you two do every last lick of the washing up,' said Frankie. 'I don't mind the money, I don't mind helping with the cooking, I don't mind the hideous noise there is going to be. I don't mind the disruption. But I am not, repeat not, having teetering towers of plates ...'

'Of course we'll wash up,' said Julia, relieved, 'won't we Lyd?'

'We *adore* washing up,' Lydia agreed.

'And we can invite *all* our friends?' Julia ventured, careful not to mention Tito specifically.

'Well, not more than thirty,' said Ray, misunderstanding. 'I don't think the floorboards could stand more than that. This house is not in the first flush of youth, you know.'

'That's no problem,' said Julia, 'because it's going to be a garden party. We are going to have glorious weather and we won't go *near* the floorboards. Oh thank you, darlings, thank you, thank you, thank you.'

CHAPTER 11

I have been feasting with mine enemy
Romeo & Juliet Act 2, Sc iii

It was late, long after the food had been served, and already as dark as it was going to get, when Lydia opened the door to find Jonathan on the doorstep. She was sure he hadn't been invited. It wouldn't be right: after all, the party was more or less to celebrate Jonathan's *not* being part of their lives any more.

She stared at him for a moment, consternation brewing in her head. Every time she saw him, something inside her went *ping!* Even the Tito factor hadn't changed that, she noted with surprise. She was glad to see him, she decided. Yes, glad.

'Jonathan!' she said, and put out her hand to him, meaning to catch his hand in hers in greeting, but he had a six-pack in one hand and a viciously thin girl hanging out of the other arm, so he just nodded at Lydia and smiled a rather crooked smile. Lydia peered in the half-light of the late-night porch. It didn't seem to be the Belly Dancer, as Julia called her. Well, he certainly got around, she thought, surprised at her own bitterness. But she spoke pleasantly enough to him, as she dropped her ungrasped hand.

'Hello,' she said. 'Sorry, no drink,' she added, when she saw the six-pack. 'My dad'll freak out. He's got a strict teetotal policy for tonight.'

'It's only Red Bull,' said Jonathan, putting his foot in the door. 'Eh, Julia invited me,' he added, defensively, as he pressed his way in. 'You look great, Lydia. Pink suits you.'

'No it doesn't,' said Lydia, playing with the ends of her hot-pink feather boa. 'Not with this hair. It's a joke. I'm wearing it *because* it doesn't suit me. It was Julia's idea. Everybody has to be un-something tonight. I'm being unsuitable.' She ended with a sad little sound that might have been meant to be a chuckle, but sounded more like a sob.

'I'm being unwelcome, so,' said Jonathan grimly.

A flood of sympathy washed through Lydia, and she forgot to feel sorry for herself for a moment. 'Uninvited,' she said, opening the door wider, 'but not unwelcome, Jonathan. Come on in. Who's your friend?'

'Maura,' said Jonathan.

Maura was teetering on impossible stilettos and seemed to need to cling on to Jonathan for balance. Lydia was tempted to say that clearly Maura was being unsteady, but she bit her tongue. She'd make a joke about it later to Julia.

Jonathan shoved the six-pack up under his armpit and pushed past Lydia. As he did so, he pressed against her and put a surreptitious hand on her hip. 'Ah, Lydia,' he whispered hoarsely, 'you and I ...'

Lydia was taken aback. From having her gesture of greeting rejected to being mauled was a leap she hadn't expected.

'Stop!' she said loudly, looking firmly at Maura and pushing his hand away. 'And that "Red Bull" of yours is Budweiser,' she added primly. 'My dad's on alcohol patrol, and if he sniffs it out, there'll be blue murder, and it'll be me and Julia that'll get blamed. So, look, would you just turn it in, Jono, there's a pet. Dad's in the dining-room – he'll take it, and you can get it again before you go home.'

'Huh!' said Jonathan and yanked Maura after him. 'You can't stop me drinking. I'm not a child.'

They tottered right past the dining room and straight out to the garden, where guests were milling about in the uncertain light of an open-mouthed wood stove. There were also tiny flickering points of light dotted about the garden, like trapped fireflies.

Beach Boys music was blaring from a speaker that Ray had fixed on the roof of the garden shed. ('It had better not rain,' he'd kept muttering as he was putting it up. 'It won't,' Julia had assured him. 'It never rains on my unbirthday.') Frankie was being DJ, which meant that the music was mostly corny sixties and seventies pop, but nobody minded. It was good party music. Everywhere, people were dancing, singing along, waving their arms above their heads, on the lawn, on the patio, on the garden path, even someone dressed entirely in bright orange, including shiny orange shoes and orange hair dye, on top of the coal bunker.

Lydia followed Jonathan and Maura out to the garden. She

needed to see what became of the Budweiser. Maura kept having to stop to wrench her ridiculous heels out of the lawn.

The girls had invited Tito, as planned, and Ray, to give him his due, hadn't said a word. Tito and Julia were squatting now, side by side, on a cement toadstool that Ray had bought one year as a joke present for Frankie. They'd all got so fond of the stupid thing that it had found a permanent home in the garden.

Tito was enchanted by the party. He'd never seen anything like it. 'Oh, Julia,' he said in a voice that was almost a whisper, 'it looks as if the sky has fallen to earth.'

'What?' asked Julia.

'The grass — it's black like the night sky,' he said, 'and look, stars are twinkling through little holes in the blackness.'

'Oh,' said Julia with a laugh, 'those! They're just nightlights in juice glasses.'

'Well, well, Julia,' said a voice above her head.

It sounded just like Jonathan, but how could it be? Surely Lydia hadn't invited him! Julia turned to look up at the speaker.

'And this is Tito,' Lydia was saying to Jonathan, looking down at Julia and Tito, hunched together in the semi-darkness of the flickering garden, and staring up now at them, their necks craning at awkward angles.

Julia and Tito both stood up, Tito reaching out a hand in his polite way to shake Jonathan's.

'What are *you* doing here?' asked Julia bluntly, fingering her canary yellow feather boa. (She was being unbecoming.)

Jonathan ignored Julia and turned to Lydia. 'I don't see anyone,' he said, 'apart from your poisonous sister.'

'How do you do,' said Tito loudly, still proffering his hand.

'Oh, there you are!' said Jonathan, pretending to have just seen Tito now, and giving his hand an unnecessarily violent shake. 'Sorry, didn't notice you. It's the dark, you don't show up against it.' He gave a barking laugh, as if to take the harm out of his remark, pass it off as a joke.

Lydia drew her breath in sharply through her teeth. Julia caught Tito's hand, giving it a protective squeeze. His long, cool fingers briefly clasped hers back and then he dropped her hand.

'What a shame you don't glow in the dark, Tito,' Julia said with forced lightness, 'like Jonathan here. He is positively radioactive, you know. A most attractive shade of green, I always think. I'm sure that's what– What's your name?' she asked, turning to Maura.

'Maura,' said Maura, with a gasp. She was still wobbling precariously and clinging to Jonathan's arm.

'What Maura finds so … engaging,' Julia finished.

'Engaging?' said Maura, flapping one hand in front of her body and tugging on Jonathan's arm with the other. 'What's engaging? We're not getting engaged, if that's what you mean. Did you tell her that, Jonathan? Honestly, you have such a mad sense of humour. Tee-hee!'

Jonathan ignored her. He was opening a can of Bud using one hand, prising at the ring with his thumb, and concentrating on not letting it fizz up.

'Cheers!' he said and put the can to his mouth.

'Jonathan, didn't Lydia say?' said Julia. 'It's a dry party. If Dad catches you with that ... It's not fair, you drink, we get into trouble.'

Jonathan took the can down from his mouth and leant over to Julia, bringing his face right up to hers. 'Lighten up,' he said, 'and give us a kiss, for old times' sake.'

He gave a beery belch and Julia stepped away from him, putting her arm involuntarily over her face to ward him off. 'Back off!' she snapped, through gritted teeth. 'Leave me be.'

Jonathan stepped back, slightly unbalanced by Julia's sudden withdrawal. He stepped right in front of Lydia, and she found herself putting a steadying hand on his elbow. He was quite drunk, but she'd only just realised it. He'd be sorry in the morning. She gave the elbow she held between her fingers a sympathetic squeeze, but Jonathan shook her off, intent on his quarrel with Julia.

'You always were such a drip, Julia,' he sneered, taking another slug from his can. 'It may be a dry party, but you could dampen it all by yourself without even trying.'

'Jonathan!' Lydia hissed, hoping to deflect him. It seemed to her that he had old scores to settle here. For the first time, it struck her that perhaps the break-up between Jonathan and

Julia hadn't been quite as Julia had portrayed it.

'A drip?' said Tito. 'What is drip?'

'A *dhreep*?' said Jonathan, mimicking Tito's accent. 'A *dhreep* is a boring person, always out to spoil everyone's fun.'

'But Julia is not boring,' said Tito, puzzled.

'Oh, so you find her entertaining? Tell me, how exactly does Julia entertain you? She won't kiss me. Maybe she kisses you? Do you like that, eh, Titus, or whatever your name is? Oh yes, I'd say you black fellows are mad for our girls, I've heard that before.'

'Jonathan!' Lydia's voice was high-pitched with anxiety. 'Don't …'

'Leave him alone, Jonathan,' said Julia tersely.

'Oh, I think maybe it is you who should leave *him* alone, Julia, my love. Strictly alone. Because, you know, you're better sticking with your own kind. Know what I mean?'

'Jonathan!' squeaked Lydia again, pulling at his jacket.

'Jonathan!' said Maura, pulling at the other side of his jacket.

Julia raised her fists, and was just about to hit Jonathan on the chest, the arms, anywhere she could reach, when Ray's voice came out of the gathering dusk.

'I'll be having that, thank you,' he said.

None of them had heard him coming up behind them, and as they spun round, Ray reached out and yanked Jonathan's can out of his hand.

'Rules are rules,' he said. 'And the rule here is that no one, regardless of age, drinks in this house tonight. Not even me. I am sure Julia and Lydia have already explained that, so which part of the concept "no one" do you not understand, Mr Walker?'

'That's mine!' shouted Jonathan and reached for the can. 'And anyway, we're not in the house, we're in the effin' garden.'

Ray dangled the can out of his reach. He was just taller than Jonathan. 'Well, I beg your pardon,' he said, 'I should have said "on these premises". Is that clear enough for you? And don't worry, I'm not going to drink it on you. As I say, I'm observing the house rule myself. You can have it when you leave. Which you will do right now. I will give it to you when you are on the other side of the front gate.'

'And take Miss University Challenge with you,' added Julia, needlessly, as Maura hadn't let go of Jonathan's arm for a moment since they'd arrived, not even when he was opening the can, not even when he was lurching forward to try to kiss Julia. She seemed to be surgically attached to him. For a brief moment, Julia found it in herself to feel sorry for him, having to lug round with him this stick insect on stilts, who appeared to be unable to stand upright without the support of his arm.

'Good night, Jonathan!' called Lydia feebly, as Ray frog-marched him and his friend through the back door and into the house. She knew it was the wrong thing to say, in the circumstances, but in spite of Jonathan's boorish behaviour and the racist things he'd said to Tito, she gave him the benefit of the doubt. Jonathan just didn't have a clue how to behave when something annoyed or upset him, that was all. And perhaps he really was missing Julia.

She sat down on the vacated cement toadstool and flung the ends of her absurd feather boa across her face. She wanted to cry, but tears wouldn't come. Nothing seemed to be going right for her. Jonathan had Maura; Julia apparently had Tito. What was the problem with Lydia?

Not noticing that Lydia was crouched by their knees, Julia turned to Tito. They looked at each other, puzzled, hurt, disconcerted by Jonathan's boorishness, but relieved that he'd gone, each one anxious to soothe the other's feelings. Their look was long and deep, and then it happened, as if scripted. He opened his arms to her, and she moved silently into his embrace. They clung together, suspended between the cold blue stars that frosted the high night sky above their heads and the little warm yellow stars that flickered out of the blackness of the garden at their feet.

The Curiosity Tree 5

F lavius shouldered his way through the crowds at the dancing area, holding his garland high above his head to keep it from getting mangled in the crowd. He squinted in the firelight and dived between bodies, trying to get a glimpse of Sun´va among the dancers. He couldn't see her anywhere. It was all contorted bodies and whooping voices, strange, freckled Celtic faces lit by the unsteady light of the fires, wild music fighting to be heard over the rumble of gossiping voices, and the odd claps of laughter from the dancers.

'Flavius!' called a sweet, high voice out of the crowd.

He swung around in the direction of the voice. She was transformed from the angry girl he had seen just a little while ago. Her forehead was creamy with calm, her expression sweet, her hair like spun gold. How could he have been so surly to her? How could anyone refuse such a creature?

She cocked her head and raised one finely arched eyebrow. 'Dance?' she said. She had forgiven him. She was giving him a second chance. '*Rince?*'

Flavius raised his garland and placed it on her head, tucking her hair in under it and curling some of the stems behind her ears, to keep it from slipping off. She laughed delightedly, a tinkly laugh, and danced her quick little fingers in among his awkward, shaking ones, settling the garland in place. Then she caught his hand in hers, raised it to shoulder height, and together they stepped onto the dancing area and lined up to dance.

Flavius struggled with the steps, twisting his head to try to see what the other dancers were doing, but she never laughed, just smiled encouragement at him and beat time with her foot to help him to understand the rhythm. As they passed each other at one point in the dance, he tried to apologise.

'About earlier,' he said, 'when you asked me to, you know, *rince*, before. Sorry.'

She had no idea what he was saying, except that she picked up the word 'dance' – *rince* – in her own language.

'*Rince*,' she repeated, nodding and smiling.

'Yes,' he said, relieved. 'I've changed my mind. Romans don't dance, but I do!' And he raised his legs in a sudden access of delight, and drew whoops from the other dancers. 'I dance!' he shouted in Latin and kicked up again.

'Hey!' yelled a dancer, 'stop kicking sand in my eyes, Roman!'

Not knowing what was being said, Flavius kicked some more.

'Keep your legs down, we don't want to see what you have under your little Roman battle-tunic!'

'I dance!' yelled Flavius, assuming that they were shouting encouragement at him.

He reached out for Sun´va, but the dancers on either side pushed him back to his place. He tried to make a break again and catch hold of Sun´va, but again they closed ranks on him, and he could feel himself being squashed by the burliness of the men around him.

'Sun´va!' he called. 'Sun´va!' But he knew his words were muffled by the clothing and bodies that were now right up against him, and he staggered, trying to gain a small space around himself. One of the men of Ireland stuck out his foot behind Flavius' heel and as he stepped back, he tripped and fell. Instantly the man whose foot he had tripped over kicked straight up, his toe catching Flavius right in the kidneys. He yelled in pain and tried to draw his sword, but they were too many for him and already he was at the bottom of a sprawling, squirming mass of bodies, his mouth full of the taste of sweat-soaked wool and the metallic tang of blood. His own blood, he thought, though he couldn't feel where it could be coming from. That was the last thought he had, as he sank under the weight of the men and felt his nostrils close and his lungs ache for air.

Rian was watching from the edge of the dancing throng. 'Troublemaker,' he muttered to himself. 'And dancing with Ultan's daughter, too. A Roman, dancing with the daughter of the chieftain!'

He went straight to the chieftain with the news that his daughter's honour was being compromised by one of the Roman vermin and that a fracas had broken out among the dancers.

Ultan swigged from his ale-cup as Rian spoke, but he listened all the same to what his steward said. He had a higher regard for his daughter's honour than did Rian, and he didn't think that dancing with a Roman would do it much damage.

That wasn't what concerned him, but clearly there was some sort of a ruckus, and it was the opportunity he had been waiting for. The last stage of his plan was about to go into action. He couldn't let it be said that Ultan the Red would countenance even the merest hint of an insult to his household, or in no time the whole country could be swarming with Romans, convinced the Celts were a pushover.

The time had come to show the Romans what the Celtic

tribes of this country were made of. They would be good and drunk by now, most of them. The same might be said of the Irish warriors, but Irish warriors fought better drunk. It was time, at last, to do battle with these unwanted visitors, and a good time too, at the darkest hour of the night, before the break of dawn, on Irish terms, and when the Romans were relaxed and not expecting an attack.

And so, on hearing Rian's argument, he sighed long and hard, drained his ale, threw the cup across the ground in a gesture of anger and followed Rian in the direction of the trouble.

Ultan quickly dispersed the scrum that had formed and at the bottom of the pile of bodies he found a young Roman soldier, not much more than a boy. The boy was bruised and breathless, but he sat up as soon as the bodies of the Irishmen were hauled off him and he said something in a splutter of sand and spittle that Ultan couldn't understand. Doubtless it was a Roman insult, since it came accompanied by a gob of spit.

Really angered now, not just going through the motions so that the battle might begin, Ultan yanked the boy up by the arm and shoved him away from the dancing area. He pushed aside his daughter, who was tugging at his sleeve, trying to calm him, trying to tell him that Flavius didn't mean any harm.

'What is this? Do you spit at Ultan the Red, chieftain of this tribe and father of this clan, you miserable Roman stripling?'

Flavius stared at Ultan, still gasping for air, wondering what he was shouting about. Perhaps he shouldn't have danced with the daughter of the chieftain. Perhaps she was promised in marriage. Flavius hung his head and tried once more to spit sand out of his mouth as discreetly as he could and to mumble some words of thanks and apology.

This appeared to enrage the chieftain even further. 'Go back to your commander!' he shouted. 'Tell him the men of Ireland will not accept this insult to our hospitality. We welcomed you as friends to our high feast, and this is how you repay us, by brawling on the floor and spitting at the chieftain. We will have our revenge on the men of Rome. Tell Tullius to prepare for battle.'

He must be very angry. Flavius had better explain. What was the word Sun´va had used for dance, earlier? He remembered it with difficulty.

'Romans – no – dance,' he said apologetically, '*Romani – no – rince*,' hoping Ultan would understand that he hadn't really wanted to dance with his daughter but she had cajoled him into it. '*Romani – no – rince*.'

'By the gods,' yelled Ultan, spittle flying in angry gobbets now from his mouth too, 'if the Romans don't dance I don't know what you were doing, but it won't be dancing you'll be this night unless it is your feet that will be dancing in the air and you hanging from the trees in this place. Get away to Tullius the centurion and tell him he has one hour of the night to prepare his troops for battle before the men of Ireland are on top of them and ready to hack them to pieces with their swords.'

Flavius still had no idea what was going on, but he knew for sure he wasn't welcome, so he gathered himself up with as much dignity as he could manage, and limped away, to find Tullius.

The Curiosity Tree 6

Sun´va had watched in dismay from the curiosity tree as Flavius picked up his leafy creation and headed off to the beach. She couldn't see anything for a while after that, except the crush of bodies at the dance. Then, just as she was about to climb down and find her tunic, she saw them: Flavius and Eva dancing on the beach, Eva wearing that absurd leafy crown thing that Flavius had made.

The swine! she thought, clambering furiously down the tree. The Roman pig! The hog! The miserable runt of an overbloated sow! To refuse her a dance and then go off with Eva. 'Romans – no – dance!' she muttered. 'I'll give you Romans no dance!'

She almost tore her tunic pulling it on angrily over her head. She caught the neckline in her torc, which she hadn't removed in case she lost it. With shaking fingers she loosened the fabric from the gold and brushed herself down. She'd see about this Roman infidel. So this is how Romans repaid Irish hospitality.

Sun´va ran to the beach, the fabric of her long festival tunic bunched in her hands to keep herself from tripping, and sidled her way into the crowds where the dancing was taking place. But the dancing had stopped. She scanned the mass of bodies, looking for Flavius and Eva so she could storm up to them and pull them apart, but she couldn't see them anywhere.

There seemed to be some sort of commotion on one

part of the beach, and she could see that her father was at the centre of it. And there was the miserable Eva, she could see her as she got closer, with her stupid wreath of flowers falling over one eye, grasping Ultan's hand and pleading with him and crying, her face blotchy and her voice harsh with tears. Ultan was shaking her off and looking away, calling to his men, rounding up his troops. There was no sign of Flavius.

'Eva!' Sun´va called over the noisy mêlée. 'What's going on? What are you crying about? And what is that thing on your hair? You must be infested with creatures. Pull it off at once or you'll get bitten by ants, or an earwig will crawl into your ear and eat your brain out, if you have one.'

Eva turned, startled, at the sound of Sun´va's voice and automatically she started to obey her sister, pulling the garland from her hair, still crying and sobbing. The honeysuckle flowers fell in polleny strands about her shoulders, and the greenery caught in her clothing, so that she looked almost as if she had drowned in the woods.

'Sun´va!' called Ultan. 'Sun´va, for the sake of the gods, get Eva out of the way. She has fallen in love with one of the Roman scum. I knew I should have married you two off long ago. Unmarried daughters bring nothing but heartache to their fathers. I can't be dealing with lovesick girls when I have to go into battle.'

'Battle?' gasped Sun´va, forgetting all about Eva's treachery with Flavius. 'A real battle?'

'No questions!' thundered Ultan. 'Go! Get Eva out of my sight before I do something I will regret.'

'Could you not …'

'Go, Sun´va daughter of Ultan, and take this snivelling

child with you.'

Sun´va pulled Eva by the elbow and walked her firmly along the beach, out of their father's way. 'It's a battle, Eva,' she said, squeezing her sister's elbow. 'Don't you understand! You can't be arguing with Ultan when he is preparing for battle.'

'But Flavius might get killed!' wailed Eva.

Sun´va's heart turned over at the thought, but she dismissed the sensation immediately. If there were to be a battle between the Irish and the Romans, then there was no doubt which side she and Eva were on, and Flavius was on the other side. Of that there was no doubt either. That was what it meant, to be the enemy.

'Don't think about it,' Sun´va said grimly to Eva. 'You said it yourself, when we met him first. You can't be getting mixed up with the enemy. Neither of us can.'

'But Flavius …'

'Is a Roman soldier,' said Sun´va, still walking Eva briskly away from where her father was gathering his men.

At the far end of the beach, away from the dancing and feasting, a clump of men sat in a circle. As Sun´va and Eva approached they could see that they had rigged up torches made of sticks wound with rags dipped in grease and tallow so that they could see what they were doing. A dice game.

One of the players must have sensed the girls behind them, because he turned. It was Cormac, his face flushed with ale and torchlight. Recognising Sun´va, he flung his arm out as if to encircle her waist, but since she was standing and he was hunkered down, he ended up encircling her thighs. This made Sun´va feel as if she were going to keel over. She swatted irritably at Cormac's arm with her hands, to make him let her go.

'Shunnevah,' said Cormac thickly. 'It's so sad.' He gave a little giggle. 'I've lost you in a bet. I have to play on to win you back.'

'What?' Sun´va was outraged. She hissed at Cormac. 'You've lost me in a …! How dare you, Cormac son of Cuan! You certainly have lost me, that's for sure, for whatever way your game goes tonight, you will never win me again. I will not be a wager, I will not be a stake at a drunken gaming table. And now, get out of here, the lot of you, at once, and report to my father. He is getting ready to go into battle against the Romans.'

'We are the fighting men of Royal Meath!' cried Cormac. 'We won't have a slip of a girl sending us into battle.'

'The battle is about to start,' shrieked Sun´va. 'Get away with you, and take your weapons with you!'

She picked up a few items from a bundle of daggers and swords and shields that had been thrown aside when the game started and pitched them into the group of men.

'Sun´va!' mewed Eva. 'Don't!'

'Ow!' yelled one of Cormac's comrades as a dagger sailed by his cheek and grazed it.

'Lucky I wasn't aiming to kill,' shouted Sun´va and threw another dagger.

The men stood up reluctantly, waving their arms before their faces to ward off any more stray daggers, and started to buckle on their weapons, lurching about in the moon- and torchlight looking for what was theirs.

'You won't send me out to battle, Sun´va, without a kiss,' wheedled Cormac, his beery breath on her cheek.

'Get off!' Sun´va pushed Cormac away from her. 'Get

away from me, you drunken beast you.'

'But we are betrothed, Sun´va,' leered Cormac.

'If we were betrothed before this night, Cormac son of Cuan, you have loosed me from my bond by losing me in a dice game. You will get no kisses from the daughter of Ultan, unless ...' She thought quickly, trying to think of an impossible condition. 'Unless you bring me the head of Tullius the centurion,' she finished triumphantly.

Eva gasped. 'Sun´va, no!'

'The head of the centurion!' The men waved their swords and slashed the air. 'By the gods, we'll get it!'

'Is that a promise?' murmured Cormac. He was pawing at Sun´va's shoulders and upper arms.

'Get off me, you drunk. Yes. It's a promise. Do you doubt the word of the daughter of Ultan the Red? You will get ten thousand kisses from the daughter of Ultan if you bring me the head of Tullius.'

'Daughter of Ultan,' said Cormac solemnly, 'I lay a *geas* on you that you keep your word, and if you do not, only evil will befall your house.'

Sun´va ignored Cormac's threat. 'Get away with you to the battlefield!' she shouted over her shoulder as she caught hold of Eva and pulled her away from the scene.

'You asked Cormac for the head of the centurion!' wailed Eva. 'Supposing he brings it to you, and you have to honour your word? You said you didn't want to marry Cormac, but you'd have to, if he brought you the head.'

'I don't believe for a moment that Cormac will get Tullius' head. He's drunk and incapable.'

But this thought didn't comfort Eva. 'No, he's laid a *geas* on you, and if you don't keep to it, we'll all be ruined.'

'Cormac has no authority to lay a *geas* on me,' said Sun´va stoutly, though she wasn't sure if that was true. She didn't know how these things worked.

'And it's a *geas* you can't keep. You can't give Cormac ten thousand kisses unless you marry him and you can't marry him because you love Flavius.'

'Love! What sort of an idea is that, you foolish girl? There is no such thing as love, except between kinspeople.'

'A husband is a kinsman,' reasoned Eva.

'Well, Fill-avius is not my husband – nor yours either.'

'But he might be.'

'Eva, you are arguing like a lunatic. I do believe Ultan is right. You've fallen for Flavius, even though you knew … You treacherous creature! What a thing it is to have a twin sister!'

CHAPTER 12

Seal up the mouth of outrage for a while,
Till we can clear these ambiguities
Romeo & Juliet Act 5, Sc iii

On the morning after the unbirthday party, Lydia trawled the garden, clearing up and checking in case any plates or glasses had been left behind. Catherine was in the next-door garden hanging out her children's clothes.

'Hey, Catherine!' Lydia called over the wall. 'I hope we didn't keep you awake last night with the music?'

'No,' Catherine called back, pinning up a pair of pyjamas. 'The children loved it. They made me leave the windows open so they could hear it. They were dancing on their beds.'

Lydia could just imagine Catherine's kids bouncing on their mattresses in time to 'Dancing Queen', their little bare feet twinkling in and out of their duvets, their pudgy little knees dimpling as they danced.

'Tito had the whole story for me,' Catherine said. She hung up a little pair of shorts and a short-sleeved cotton shirt. 'It was nearly as good as being there, the way he told it, the food, the music, the people, everything. He said you had jars of starlight on the ground. Sometimes, I don't know what that boy is talking about, the way he describe things.' She shook her head, but she smiled at the same time. 'Stars in jars! Really, that what he said.'

'I'm sorry we couldn't invite everyone,' Lydia said, stuffing the last stray napkin into the refuse-sack she was carrying, and coming to the wall to talk more easily. 'Only Dad said we had to keep the numbers down. Are you all settling in OK?' Funny how this question, which had seemed so silly when she'd asked it of Tito the other day in the shop, seemed perfectly appropriate now.

'Oh yes, pretty good,' said Catherine. She stretched to the highest part of the line with the last pair of socks. 'We had no more trouble, not since your father spoke to those people.'

'My father?' said Lydia. 'What did you say?'

Catherine didn't answer. Instead she said, 'Come in for a cup of my coffee. The children went with my neighbour to the park, and I am going to have a little time for myself. I got good coffee from Kenya, much better than you buy in the shops here. Delicious.'

'Thanks,' said Lydia. 'I'd love to.'

'Bring your twin,' said Catherine. 'Tito's not home, though,' she added with a sly grin. 'See you in a minute, OK?'

The door of the neighbouring house opened into a dark and spicy cave. There were muffled sounds everywhere, as if creatures who wore carpet slippers lived in the walls. Julia and Lydia looked around them curiously. They'd never been in this house all the time the Phillips family had lived there.

'Welcome,' said Catherine's voice, out of the gloom of the hall, as she closed the door.

Lydia started. 'Oh, Catherine, it's you!'

'Who else?' said Catherine. 'Me and Patrick.'

She opened the door into a large front room, and they could see from the light that flooded out of that room that she had the baby in her arms, his little head lolling against her soft shoulder.

'This is where we eat,' she said, ushering the girls in.

The room was large and bright, the walls painted in pure white and the flimsy curtains on the big bay window drawn right back. In their house, the equivalent room was the family living room, with sofas and a television and bookcases, but here two long canteen-type tables with brown, shiny, wood-effect surfaces and straight black metal legs formed a T in the centre of the bare-floored room. Around the tables stood an assortment of chairs: a few modern plastic bucket chairs, some stained with paint or oil, two or three old-fashioned kitchen chairs, painted in bright but chipped primary colours, and a couple of swivelling office chairs, one of them gashed across the seat, which grinned a great dirty yellow foam-rubber grin. All around the walls were posters, some charts of Irish wild flowers and animals, some giving information about joining the credit union, crossing the road safely, vaccination pro-grammes, how to get your residence permit renewed.

'I put up the posters,' said Catherine, proudly. 'I got a job now, you know. Here, you take him for a minute, would you?'

She handed the baby to a surprised Julia, who'd never held a baby before. She held him gingerly, out from her body, in case she squashed him, and tried to look into his eyes, but they were closed, his small dark moths of eyelids drawn down.

'A job?' said Lydia, pulling out two chairs for herself and Julia. 'I thought you wouldn't be allowed to work. Here, Jule, sit down, you won't be so likely to drop him.'

'Oh, this is not a paid job. It's at my church.'

Catherine had moved up to the table that formed the bar of the T and started to set up a little gas stove with a small battered saucepan on it.

'I make my coffee here. It get crowded in the kitchen, at this time of day, everyone cooking,' she explained.

'What kind of job?' asked Julia, settling Patrick on to her lap.

'We have a centre for African people,' said Catherine, lighting the gas. 'I help with translating documents for people. Sometimes I go with them to official places if their English is not good. That sort of thing. I am an industrial chemist, really, but it is nice to help people, and, you know, it is better to go there and do things for people than to sit here all day, worrying about my husband. And besides, that's where I get my coffee. You have to have something fine in your life, even if you poor, and in my life – besides my kids, of course – it's coffee.'

'An industrial chemist?' said Lydia. 'You mean you work in a lab, bubbling things up in test tubes? You shouldn't be poor.'

'Well,' said Catherine, 'right now I'm just an asylum seeker, like everyone else here. The only thing I bubble up these times is my coffee.'

A silence fell, and the girls could again hear the small, muffled sounds of life from other rooms, other families living in small spaces.

'Is your husband here?' asked Julia, stroking Patrick's head lightly with her fingertips. She was getting the hang of babies, she thought.

'No,' said Catherine. 'Every day, we wait to hear from him, but since we arrived, nothing.'

'Since you arrived?' said Julia. 'You mean, not even when the baby was born; he doesn't know?'

Unconsciously, Julia held Patrick closer to her body, settling her arm more comfortably under and around him. She'd thought a baby would be wriggly and squirmy and rather damp, like a bag of squid, but he made a warm, firm bundle, not at all as she'd expected, very soothing to hold.

'He is a doctor. He knew when the baby would come, but no, I haven't had a phone call from him, or a letter, e-mail, nothing. I don't know if he alive, even.'

'Oh, Catherine!'

'Well, we just hope. I tell the children stories about him, so they don't forget, because maybe they never see their daddy again. But at least we safe here, now. Patrick was born here. That means he can be an Irish person, and they will probably let me stay too, because I must bring him up, and maybe the other children get to stay also, I'm not sure, we hope, we hope.'

'Oh, I *hope* they do,' said Lydia. 'And I hope your husband makes it.'

'Yes,' said Catherine. 'We all hope. *Your* daddy,' she went on, looking up from her task, 'he's a good man.'

'He is?' said Julia.

'Uh-hm. He came and spoke to those people who were making the riot – remember? – the day when I loaned the milk from your mother.'

Lydia and Julia stared at each other. Their father hadn't even been there, as far as they knew.

'We thought he was already at work that morning,' said Lydia, carefully.

'Oh, he dressed for work,' said Catherine, 'in that suit he wears, with his little leather – what you call that square case they carry, businessmen?'

'Briefcase,' said Lydia.

'Briefcase,' said Catherine, nodding, 'but he stopped out there, at the corner' – she pointed out the window to the nearby junction – 'and he turned back and he go right up to the guy with the horn and he start waving his arms. I don't know what he said, but it worked. They stopped, they went home.'

A delicious smell of coffee was starting to rise up from Catherine's stove.

'He most probably threatened them with terrible things,' Catherine went on. 'That's what it looked like, the way he was shouting at them. Oh, he was magnificent! I saw him, through that window there, after I come home with the milk. Your mother got one good man, there. She should give him that love bean.'

'Give him the love bean?' said Julia. 'But you gave it to her, she can't just give it away. That would be, like, a betrayal of your kindness.'

'Oh no, no,' said Catherine. 'You pass it on; that way, you pass the love around. That make the world better. Tito gave it to me, when I helped him with some of his paperwork for the asylum process, I gave it to your mother, to be a friend to her, she can give it to someone she loves. That's how it goes.'

'I didn't know that,' said Julia. 'I thought it was just between two people.'

'Ah then, maybe you don't understand much about love,' said Catherine. 'It's never just between two people.'

She came towards them now, with two small china cups, tiny, almost like doll's crockery, with little gold patterns on them, and set them down, steaming and fragrant, in front of the girls.

'I'll take Patrick,' she said, holding out her arms for him. 'Babies and hot drinks don't mix too good.'

As Julia handed him to his mother, Patrick's eyes opened and he yawned a wide, gummy yawn.

'Hello, baby,' said Catherine.

'Tell me more about Tito,' Julia begged her.

'Tito,' said Catherine, with a smile in her voice. 'You like Tito, yes?'

'You know I do,' Julia said.

'I think you like him too,' Catherine said to Lydia.

'Well … I …' Lydia stumbled, blushed.

'But I think maybe you like someone else too, hmm?'

Lydia stared. Was this woman psychic or what?

'He a good boy, Tito,' Catherine said. 'He will make a fine man.'

'Yes, I know that,' said Julia.

'But he's sad,' said Catherine, expertly turning the baby close in towards her body, to feed him. 'He's had a hard time.'

'He told me about his sister,' Julia said quickly, 'how she died.'

'Died?' said Lydia. 'His sister is dead?'

'Yes,' said Catherine, 'and his father. He killed by the army people in his country. Something about politics. He was on the wrong side. He told you why he left, why he came to Ireland?'

'No,' said Julia.

'One reason was to get his little sister away from that man they want her to marry.'

'Cruel,' said Julia fiercely, looking at Lydia.

'What?' said Lydia, lost.

'No,' said Catherine unexpectedly. 'The uncle, he try to do his best. When Tito's father is killed, the uncle, he has all these children to look after. He's not a rich man, how can he feed all his brother's children as well as his own? So if someone want to marry the girl, well, that's one less mouth to feed. That's all.'

'Oh,' said Julia. 'I see. Well, I suppose …'

'Listen to this one,' Catherine said with a smile, gesturing with her head to the baby at her breast. He snuffled and suckled, snuffled and suckled, small, wet, happy sounds, like a tiny brown piglet. Julia thought it was the warmest sound she'd ever heard.

When they got home, the twins told Frankie about the love bean being transferable, and how Catherine thought maybe Ray deserved it for being so 'magnificent' about the trouble in the street.

'For magnificence in the face of street rioting,' Frankie said, laying it before him that night after dinner. 'Your secret is out.'

'What? Oh, that,' said Ray. 'Well, I just told them I wouldn't have riots near my house. I said I'd rung the guards and if they weren't gone by the time the police arrived that I'd take a civil action against them.'

'An action?' asked Lydia, astonished.

'Yes. That always frightens people. I told them I was a senior counsel, and I'd never lost a case. I said I'd sue them personally for a million pounds each. Most of them left.'

'Dad!' said Julia. 'You're just a crummy little solicitor with a conveyancing practice.'

'Less of the "crummy little", please,' said Ray.

'I hope you impressed on them that this is a *residential* area,' said Julia.

'I most certainly did,' said Ray. 'Why else do you think I wanted to stop that damned riot? We can't have that sort of thing going on around here.'

'No,' said Julia emphatically, 'we can't. Think of what it'd do to property values.'

'Exactly. *And* I said, of course, also, that we are decent people who wouldn't condone racist violence.'

'You did?' Julia stared.

'Well, what do you think, Julia?' her father asked, serious now.

'I don't know what to think,' said Julia.

'In that case,' said Ray, 'maybe you might consider, just for once, giving me the benefit of the doubt?'

'Eh,' said Julia, in a small voice, 'yes. Of course. I …'

'Because there's a world of difference, you know,' Ray went on, 'between objecting to having a hostel next door and violence against innocent people. Just because I care about the value of this house doesn't mean I'm going to put up with the intimidation of unfortunate people who have nowhere else to live. Have you got that, Julia?'

'Yes,' said Julia. 'Sorry.'

'Here,' she added, after a moment, 'have the love bean.' She picked it up, from where Frankie had laid it in front of Ray, and pressed it into his hand.

'I'm allowed back into the human race, then, am I?' asked Ray, fingering the dark, smooth surface of the love bean.

'For the moment,' said Julia with a small grin. She leant her forehead against his for a moment and said softly, 'Sorry, Dad.'

Ray silently tipped the love bean from his palm onto hers and closed her fingers over it.

Julia shook her head. 'No, it's for you,' she whispered, 'from Mum.'

'You have it,' he said. 'You'll find a use for it.'

The Curiosity Tree 7

Igh in her curiosity tree, at the edge of the forest and overlooking the beach, Sun´va blew on the war-trumpet, calling the Irish to battle. The horrendous noise she blew out over the beach sent shivers up her own spine.

'What sort of a demented creature makes such terrible music?' Flavius asked.

'It's war,' Tullius answered. 'You were right. All that feasting and carousing – I knew it was too good to be true. That terrible music, as you call it, is announcing a battle.'

He sighed as he buckled on his leather armour. He had only a small scouting troop, sent out to explore the island to the west of Britain. They were armed, surely, but they were not really prepared for a full-scale battle. Tullius' men were brave and highly trained, but he didn't believe they had much chance against these wild Celts, who after all were fighting on their native soil, and could call on reinforcements from the gods knew where.

'You're a great soldier, Tullius,' said Flavius, 'one of the best. You'll lead us to victory for sure over these mad Celts.'

'I've had enough of warfare, Flavius,' he said. 'I've killed more men than you've had hot dinners, and I'd hoped to finish my days in a sunny vineyard in Lazio, not to spill out my guts on an Irish beach.'

Sun´va blew and blew, and the sound of the trumpet

was repeated and repeated, a wailing, gut-strangling sound.

Terrible as the noise of the war-trumpet was, it was followed by a worse sound – the raucous screech of a huge crow that dipped suddenly out of the dawn-streaked sky and flew low over the beach, its wings making a wind like the breath of death and its croaking like the very voice of evil.

'What's that?' Flavius asked.

'Only a bird,' said Tullius.

'It's the Morrigan,' Sun´va whispered to herself, awestruck. 'The goddess of battle, come to support us in our fight against the Romans.'

'Well,' Tullius went on, opening his arms to embrace the young soldier. 'The blessings of Mars on you, son, and may Jupiter protect you.'

Tullius thumped Flavius on the back and then moved off among his men, to tell them that the feast had ended, and it was time to do battle.

With quick, tense, almost automatic movements, the soldiers set aside their food and drink or emerged from their leather tents. They gathered their weapons in near-silence, put on their armour, and lined up soberly, their shields held at precise angles and their swords drawn and held before them.

Only yards away, across the gleaming sands, the Celts lined up opposite them, jostling and yelling, their blood-curdling cries drowning the sea's incessant hiss. Sun´va looked down on the sober lines of Romans to one side and the heaving mass of Celts to the other, and she was afraid, but what she was afraid of, she hardly knew.

As if out of nowhere, Manus the druid appeared then on the sands between the two sides, a ghostly figure in the scant light. His wispy beard blew over his shoulder in the sea breeze.

'It's Neptune!' one of the Romans whispered to Flavius. 'He has just now walked out of the sea.'

'No,' said Flavius. 'It …'

'I tell you,' said Aurelius. 'Look at his long beard!'

'If it is a god, it is a god of the Celts, for look how he is dressed, like one of them.' The rumour flew through the Roman ranks. 'The Celts have summoned a god to their aid. We can't win against a god.'

'Rubbish!' shouted Tullius when this rumour reached his ears. 'What nonsense! It is an old white-haired man, not a god. The Celts have no gods stronger than our gods, and we have observed all the rituals correctly. Our gods are pleased with our observances; they will be with us tonight. And anyway, that's Manus the druid. I met him myself earlier today.'

Manus raised his arms to the fading moon, and both armies fell silent. Sun´va put down her war trumpet so that Manus could be heard. The crow that had been hovering over the beach settled on a rock near the water's edge.

'Good people!' called Manus. 'Good people all!' He addressed the Romans as well as the Irish, though they didn't understand a word he said. 'Why go to battle on this night that is sacred to the god Lu? Why tarnish our feasting now with the blood of newly made friends? If there is retribution to be paid, if there is a dispute to be settled, let it be done in a civil manner. Let us talk before it is too late.'

Murmurs came from the Irish warriors, murmurs that crescendoed to a dull roar of dissent.

'Well, if ye will not parley, then,' said Manus the wise,

'will ye at least restrict the conflict to the leaders?'

The crow rose up suddenly with a flap from the rock where it had perched and went wheeling and screeching over the beach again.

Murmurs arose again. 'It's the Morrigan,' the Irish muttered, pointing at the crow. 'She's come to warn us not to make peace.'

Manus waved his arms for silence.

'I look about me,' he said, 'and on both sides I see cruel weapons and battle-ready men. I see two armies that are evenly matched in numbers, in weapons and in valour. If ye fight this night, it will be a long battle and a bloody one …'

A cheer went up from the Irish army.

'… and it will end with the white sands of this place turning red with the blood of generations. Children will be left fatherless and women weeping. The remains of the harvest will rot in the fields for want of men to gather it in. What kind of an insult is that to Macha, goddess of the earth, to let her crops spoil and to defile her waterways with the blood of the valiant?'

'Give over, old man,' called one of Ultan's men. 'We are soldiers, trained to fight, and fight we will! You pray and we fight. That's how things are.'

From her perch in the oak tree, Sun´va sounded her trumpet out triumphantly over the heads of the warriors.

'Let us get down to battle!' shouted one of the Romans, tired of all this talk in a foreign tongue. 'We are ready to meet them!'

Sun´va blew on the trumpet again, and it was as if the wind held a giant blade of grass in the crack between her thumbs and blew into the sharp edge of it. Again the crow, the one the people said was the Morrigan herself come to spur the Irish on to win, went screeching and jabbering up the beach.

'Very well,' said Manus and lowered his arms. 'The blessings of the gods on ye all.' He withdrew as silently and as mysteriously as he had come.

And again came the trumpet's harsh bellow, like a cow in labour.

There was a moment's silence after the trumpet call died away, and then the two armies came surging forward to meet each other over the moonlit sand, whooping and yelling encouragement to each other and insults at the enemy. From her position in the tree, Sun´va could see what the Romans couldn't: even as they charged, the ranks of the Irishmen opened and the war-chariots came dashing through, led by Ultan astride his great chieftain's chariot. Wheels churned up the sands, horses whinnied with fear and excitement, and the charioteers astride the shafts yelled as they sped into the ranks of the Romans. They knocked soldiers off their feet, rolled over the bodies on the ground, cracked men's bones under their wheels, and still they surged forward. The swordsmen and javelin throwers who stood in the chariots behind the charioteers slashed out indiscriminately behind and before and to the side, so that clear areas quickly opened up around the chariots, as the Roman foot soldiers backed off, out of the range of flailing Irish weapons.

Sun´va blew excitedly, victoriously, but as she lowered the trumpet from her lips, she could see that the Irish had begun to lose the initial advantage of having horses in the fight. Instead of backing away from the chariots, some of the bravest of the Romans attacked the horses with their swords, and their gashed chests opened up like corn sacks being slit to release their contents. The horses slithered in their own blood as it poured from their bodies, and they staggered to the ground, pitching the charioteers and swordsmen forward, right into the path of Roman swords. All the Romans had to do in some cases was hold their swords up and the charioteers impaled themselves in their headlong fall.

Ugh! It was a horrible sight, horrible to see animals in agony, horrible to see Irish warriors falling on Roman swords, horrible even to see Roman bodies crushed by out-of-control chariots. Sun´va forgot about her trumpet for a while and just watched in terrified suspense. She could see Ultan, still upright in his chariot, flailing all around him, swiping limbs and heads off with his sword, and she could see Tullius, on the edge of the battle, shouting orders to his men, urging them to move this way, that way. But there was no sign of the boy Flavius. He was young, it was maybe his first battle, he'd probably been crushed to death in the first charge, poor boy. Her heart contracted. What a waste! She couldn't see Cormac anywhere either, and she wondered if he'd bothered to join the battle at all. She wouldn't put it past him to be hiding somewhere till the fighting was over. Or maybe he'd been killed too, and he'd be no loss.

As the battle wore on, the stench of blood mixed with horse dung hung in the air like a putrid gas. Warriors reeled about with weapons stuck in their bodies, the blood spurting from their wounds, unable to die, unable even to fall to the ground, so tightly packed were the troops. As blood spurted from arteries, arcs of it rose through the air over the battle scene, so that it seemed as if the very sky was bleeding, raining blood down onto the heads of the warriors so that they were blinded by blood and could see only through a red mist. And still the battle went on, the screams of agony mingling with the horses' frightened neighs and the warriors' guttural yells of anger and encouragement.

As dawn strengthened in the eastern sky, Sun´va spied Manus coming gliding over the sands towards the battling warriors.

'Listen to me!' he called over the roar of battle and the cries of the wounded, animal and human, still moving towards the fighting.

What a foolish old man! He'd be killed! Sun´va gave a series of loud, short blasts on the trumpet, to alert the armies to Manus' presence, and, miraculously, they seemed to understand, for a quiet descended over the battlefield.

'Halt!' called Manus again. 'Listen! It is no dishonour to halt the battle, to take a pause. Halt!'

Slowly the living put down their swords and used bloody fingers to wipe away the blood that dripped from their hair into their eyes and down their faces.

'Listen to me!' called Manus again. 'Neither side is going to win this battle. The only victor here today is death. The way to the Otherworld will be clogged this night with the spirits of the men of Ireland and the men of Rome. The funeral fires will burn for hours, and the stench of burning flesh will lie heavily upon this bay. The women and children will have a sorry task and it is a hard winter they will face this year with no husbands and fathers to fight off the wolves that come howling down from the hills in times of hunger. And there will be hunger in Irish homesteads come the solstice, for the crops will not have been gathered, and the winter stores will be depleted. It is a sorry day for the people of this place. And if this battle continues to the end, there will be no one left to bury the dead and mourn the lost.'

A ripple of murmurs went through the remains of the two armies. Even the Romans could hear the sorrow in his voice.

'Once again, I put it to you, people of Ultan and people of Tullius. Let your leaders fight in single combat to settle this dispute and leave us the warriors who survive to be fathers to the orphans and gatherers of the crops and protectors of the weak.'

He turned to the Romans and held up a single finger of one hand, and a single finger of the other, to indicate single combat, and Tullius understood. Sun´va could see the tiniest nod of agreement from him.

Murmurs surged again, and warriors on both sides waved their swords weakly in defiance. But the murmurs died quickly away. The warriors were too weary to argue.

'So!' called Manus, raising his voice in authority. 'I call upon Ultan the Red to come forward. I call upon Tullius the centurion to come forward. And I call upon you both to fight to the death, to settle this dispute. Before you do, I declare that if Tullius dies' – he let the hand on the Roman side drop and waved victoriously with the hand on the Irish side – 'and the Irish win, the Romans shall depart from this place and leave us in peace,' – he made a sweeping gesture out to sea with the Roman hand, and then pointed at the rising sun and drew his pointing finger across the sky and down to the western horizon – 'before the Lunasa sun that now rises over the sea has set over the plains. And if our beloved chieftain Ultan dies and the Romans win' – he did his mime act again, now in reverse – 'the men of Ireland shall let them pass unmolested on their way to the interior of the country to look for gold or precious metals or to find other armies to fight or whatever it is that they are looking for. Is it agreed?'

The murmur rose up again on both sides. Sun´va held her breath. If Ultan agreed, he stood a high chance of being killed, her father, killed! It was unthinkable! What would they do without him? Who would be chieftain then? She'd have to marry Cormac so he could be chieftain. She shuddered at the thought.

'Agreed!' called Ultan and he stepped forward, brandishing his sword which already dripped with blood. His hair was matted with blood and sweat and sand, but he stood fearlessly facing the enemy, his sword already raised.

There was a moment of silence. Sun´va shifted her stiffening body on her branch. They were waiting for her to indicate the Celtic warriors' agreement. She lifted the trumpet to her quivering lips, and gave a sad little blow. It came out as a low wail, and Sun´va's heart wailed too.

'Agreed!' called Tullius in his own language, for he had got the gist of Manus' intervention, and he too stepped forward.

Sun´va gathered her breath again, and gave a brisk blast on the trumpet also for his agreement.

'Have I the word of both sides that the outcome shall be settled by the combat of Tullius and Ultan?' Manus asked.

'Yes,' said Ultan's men wearily, and threw their bloody

weapons on the ground before them.

Manus looked questioningly at the battle-weary Romans. They understood they were being asked for consent, and they too flung their weapons on the ground.

As the leaders came forward to face each other, silence fell over the two depleted armies. So quiet was it that Sun´va could have sworn she heard the moment at which the tide turned, and the sea started its long, slow journey back up the bloodied sands.

'Go on, Ultan,' she whispered, watching as her father moved forward to meet the centurion. 'Don't die! Your people need you. Kill the Roman, kill him!'

The combat was short and cruel. Ultan slashed and Tullius slashed back, his sword wavering in his exhausted hand. Ultan slashed again, and Tullius fell.

Both armies watched in silence. Tullius lay motionless on the sands between them. Sun´va watched also, counting her breaths to calm herself, waiting to see if he should regain consciousness, make the slightest movement, but still he lay at Ultan's feet.

The huge black crow the people said was the Morrigan flew silently down and landed for a moment on Ultan's shoulder, as if to congratulate him on his victory. Then she rose again with a thunderous flapping of wings and flew up and up and up until she was just a tiny black speck in the sky.

Victory! Sun´va hardly dared to think the word, but what else could it be? After all the fighting and the death and the destruction, that single sword strike of Ultan's had finished it – finished Tullius, finished the battle.

Manus reappeared, and gestured again to the Romans

that they should depart by sunset. This confirmed Ultan's victory. Sun´va gave a wild, triumphant blast on the trumpet, and then Flavius and another soldier came forward quickly and moved the body of Tullius into the Roman camp.

Flavius! So he'd survived the battle. Sun´va gave one last joyful blast on the trumpet. There could be no better outcome: victory to Ultan and Flavius still alive.

CHAPTER 13

This bud of love, by summer's ripening breath,
May prove a beauteous flow'r when next we meet
Romeo & Juliet Act 2, Sc ii

Tito was stunned by the cappuccino bar down at the sea, where Julia had insisted on taking him. He stared around him at the stainless steel counter with its elaborate stainless steel espresso machine and its huge metal-weave basket piled high with lustrous oranges, at the bright orange lacquered chairs and the polished floor and the shining plate-glass window, through which you could see the wide, blue expanse of the Irish Sea. He was so mesmerised by all this gleaming, angular beauty that he forgot to order, until Julia nudged him and pointed to the pale, edgy, black-clothed waitress who was looming by their table.

'Juice,' he said at last. 'Please.'

'Orange juice, mango and passion fruit juice, apple juice, cranberry juice, mixed berry juice, wheatgrass juice?' asked the waitress, with exaggerated weariness.

'Oh, I think I'll just have coffee,' he said, defeated by this array of choice.

'Regular coffee, espresso, cappuccino or latte? Or flavoured with hazelnut, chocolate, rum or Irish cream?'

Tito shook his head and looked at Julia to rescue him.

'Two cappuccinos, please,' said Julia briskly. 'You'll like cappuccino,' she added to Tito. 'It's not as good as the stuff Catherine makes, but it's good.'

'With?' asked the waitress, tapping her pencil on her notepad.

'With what?' asked Julia.

'Chocolate sprinkles,' snapped the waitress.

'Of course,' Julia said, dismissively, to the waitress. 'What?' she said then, seeing how Tito stared at her.

'I wish I could be like that.'

'How do you mean? How am I?'

'Slotted in.'

Julia spooned chocolaty froth from the top of her cappuccino into her mouth and watched the way Tito's long, dark fingers flitted in and out as he opened and closed his fists in frustration. Black people's hands are so much more interesting, she thought. Being white is so boring. She wondered if she should voice these thoughts, but worried then whether she might sound patronising again. She decided against it.

'Slotted in to what?' she asked instead.

'The jigsaw,' said Tito, opening one fist again and spreading his palm on the table top so that his hand made a large, dark starfish on the pale beechwood surface. 'You're part of the right jigsaw. You're comfortable in your place. But I'm like a piece from the wrong jigsaw. Always a jagged fit. And always, there are people who say, What's *he* doing in this jigsaw? He don't fit. Let's put him back in his own box.'

Julia laughed, though she knew Tito wasn't making a joke. 'Have you applied for refugee status?' she asked then, trying out the new language she had learnt from Catherine.

'Yes,' said Tito. 'I'm waiting to hear. It's mostly waiting, being a refugee. You queue, you wait, you wait, you meet someone, you wait, you fill a form, you wait, you queue again, you wait, you fill another form, you wait and wait and wait. Eighty, ninety percent don't get it – don't get refugee status. You never know, never, never know when they will ask to see you, what they will say, if you will get deported, sent back to the army, to be killed.'

Julia turned her spoon softly in what was left of her cappuccino.

'Killed? In a war, you mean?'

'No. *They'll* kill me,' Tito said, 'like they … killed … my father.'

'The army?'

'Yes, it was the army. They killed him, because he wouldn't fight with them.'

'Catherine told us. Not the whole story, just that the army shot your dad.'

Tito's eyes pooled with sudden tears.

'Sorry,' said Julia.

'No, no,' said Tito. 'I'll tell you.' He dabbed at his eyes with the thick orange napkin and took a few deep breaths as if to reclaim his composure. 'One morning,' he said, in a strange, formal tone, as if telling a story he'd often had to tell, 'he went out to the fields, my father, and he never came home. Later, I went to find him. He was lying on his face, in the field. The flies were already laying their eggs in the wound on the back of his head. There wasn't much blood, only some that had … you know, got thick and sticky around the hole in his head.'

'Congealed,' Julia croaked.

'Yes. I had to dig his grave myself. The earth was hard and dry and it took me all day, what was left of it. My hands got cut and one of my nails came off, I exhausted myself. But what could I do? It was hot. He had to be buried. Then I went home in the evening and told my mother.'

Tito clenched the hand that lay on the table between them into a fist.

'Oh my God!' whispered Julia.

'It was a Tuesday,' Tito went on, looking away from her, out the window, out to sea. His voice had got very low, as if he were talking to himself. She had to lean close to hear him. 'I remember, because that was the day she went to market to sell her eggs. She was coming singing along the road, swinging her basket, as I came in from the field. I went to meet her. I took the basket from her, and I told her what had happened.'

'Oh, Tito,' Julia whispered, but he didn't seem to hear.

'She sat down in the dust of the road and wept, my little

mother. In her best market-day dress, to sit in the dust! I was more shocked by that, I think, than by seeing my father stretched out and dead. That's when my heart broke, to see my mother sitting in the dust and crying as if nothing mattered any more except that he was dead and now she had no husband and her children had no father.'

Julia tried to imagine what it would be like to find her father stretched in death, flies buzzing about his head, what it would be like to see her mother weep. She couldn't.

'So I left. I had to go. They'd be back for me. My mother knew it, she said I must go. I took Nkemi with me, to save her from that old man who wanted her, and then see what happened to her.'

'It wasn't your fault.'

'It was,' he insisted.

For a long time, they sat silently, sipping their coffee from time to time.

'You see, I thought, it is not nice for a girl, twelve, to marry a man, fifty-three.'

'Fifty-three!' Julia breathed. 'That's *prehistoric!*'

'Anyway,' Tito went on, 'twelve is too young for, you know … having babies. She was very small, slim. It could have killed her. She was so pretty, so merry, always laughing, singing, skipping about. Her eyes sparked.'

'Sparkled,' said Julia.

'Yes,' said Tito, 'sparkled. Like the stars. So I said, "Nkemi, let's go to Ireland." We know about Ireland. We went to a school with Irish nuns. It is a green country, they tell us, with cattle and little damp hills and the people are friendly. Everyone has enough to eat and there is no war there, or not much, only in one area. So I said to Nkemi, "Sister, you come with me, perhaps you find a better man to marry overseas." So she came. It *is* my fault. Maybe that man would be good to her, maybe she would not have babies till she's older. But now she will never have a baby. I took her away from her mother and her country. I wanted to keep her safe but I only put her in danger.'

'It's not your fault,' Julia said again.

'Maybe not,' he said, but she could see he only said it to please her.

She didn't know what to say next. She didn't think she could bear to hear any more about what had happened to Tito, that story that he had to carry around with him, would have to carry for the rest of his life. Nothing in her experience had prepared her for this sort of conversation.

'And now?' she said, feebly. 'What do you want now?'

'A normal life. That's all. Normality. Safety.'

'Normal? What is that? What do you mean?'

'Like your family.'

'We're normal?' said Julia. 'And that's good?'

She thought about her sarcastic remarks about the Phillipses who had lived next door. She thought of herself and Lydia, squabbling over the washing-up, arguing about Jonathan, stealing each other's lipsticks, swapping books, writing stupid party invitations, playing imaginary violins when their dad started with one of his 'when I was your age' kicks, calling their mum by her first name just because they knew it irritated her. She'd always thought of her life as boring, predictable, uneventful, and safe, above all, safe. She used the word 'safe' as a term of abuse. But for Tito the word 'safe' meant being in a place thousands of miles from your own people and everyone you loved, speaking a foreign language all the time, and in constant fear of a knock on the door, an official-looking envelope, but still safe – for now at least, the army wasn't going to come to shoot you in a field.

'Yes,' said Tito. 'That is why I like to live next door to you. The washing flaps on the clothesline, voices come through the windows, people laughing, arguing, your mother burns the potatoes and they make a charred smell.'

Julia wrinkled her nose.

'Catherine too,' he went on. 'She's afraid, always afraid, like me. But she makes a normal life with her kids. She tries to potty-train the little one, she sings the baby to sleep, I help the older boy with his homework. Normal, see? That's what I want. To be like you and your family – you eat, you give parties, you cut roses. To sing a baby to sleep, that's all I want for my life, to cut roses, burn potatoes. That's all.'

Julia had never sung a baby to sleep. It had never occurred

to her as something she might want to do. It was an effort to see it Tito's way, but she thought then of the warm parcel that Patrick had made in her arms, and she thought maybe she understood.

Tito's hand came down over his face again, in the gesture he used when he was weary. He dropped his hand onto the table top, and Julia reached out and touched it lightly with her fingertips.

After a while, she said, a little sheepishly, 'I've got something for you, Tito.'

'Oh?' said Tito. 'For me? Like the roses for Nkemi?'

'Not exactly. It's this.' Julia drew her fist out of her pocket and turned it over as Tito had done that day in their kitchen. She opened her fingers one at a time, and there, in the middle of her palm, was the love bean, gleaming with its dull sheen. She held it out towards him.

'But ... this is your mother's?' he said. 'Is it from your mother?'

'No,' said Julia. 'When we heard, me and Lydia – Catherine told us – that you can pass it on, we told Frankie and she passed it ... well, it's a long story, but it ended up with me. And now, I am giving it to you.'

'To me?'

'Tito, do you want the love bean?' Julia asked. She was still holding it out on her palm, offering it to him.

'Of course,' he said. 'Of course.'

He picked it out of her hand and turned it over and over, running the pad of his thumb over its familiar polished surface. It was dense, heavy and very smooth.

'Thank you, Julia,' he said, in that formal way he had. 'I am honoured.'

'But I want you to keep it, now,' she said.

'To keep it always?'

Always? Who could think about always? Tito might not even be here in a year's time. Lydia was the one who went in for Love, Big and Serious and For Ever. 'Love is not love/Which alters when it alteration finds,' she would quote grandly, adding that Love was everlasting and immutable as the stars. Julia was more sceptical. And anyway, the stars are far from immutable, as she pointed out to Lydia.

'Well,' Julia said now, 'maybe there will be a time when you need to pass it on. But for now, let's keep it for ourselves, Tito.'

'Ourselves,' he said. Then he nodded and closed his fingers over the love bean. 'Yes. For ourselves. For now.'

The Curiosity Tree 8

Later that morning, while the women were moving among the Celtic dead on the beach, preparing their bodies for cremation, Flavius was bathing the wounds of a comrade in the sea. Cormac, son of the king of Meath, came stealthily into the Roman camp.

'Where is Tullius the centurion?' he shouted.

Flavius looked up.

'Tullius the centurion,' Cormac demanded again.

Flavius looked at him curiously, but it didn't occur to him that Cormac meant no good, so he pointed to where he had left Tullius' body. He turned back then to his work with Marcus, murmuring encouragement to his wounded friend.

Behind him, Cormac let an ear-splitting yell like a wolf howling at the moon, and there followed the swift sound of a sword slicing the air. Flavius spun around, in time to see Tullius' poor head roll away gently from the severed nerves and sinews and veins and arteries of his neck, the tongue falling out of his mouth in a grotesque caricature of Tullius' living face.

'No!' roared Flavius. 'No!'

Leaving his semi-conscious comrade half in the water, half on the sand, Flavius leapt to his feet and went for Cormac, blinded with rage and terror. But Cormac had a sword, and Flavius, coming from washing Marcus' wounds, had only his fists. Cormac held the sword out and waved it to keep Flavius at bay.

'I claim the head of Tullius!' he taunted. 'The head is my trophy.'

Flavius didn't understand a word of this except 'Tullius', and to hear the name of his poor dead commander on the lips of this scoundrel made him wretched as well as furious. He made several attempts to bypass the flailing sword, but he could not get near Cormac.

Cormac made one final, whacking cut in the air with the sword in Flavius' direction and then he swung around and plunged its point into the gaping neck-stump of Tullius' head. With the head of the centurion impaled on it, he waved his sword triumphantly, practically under Flavius' nose, and he was shouting and laughing. Then he turned tail and made for the Irish end of the wide beach, yelling for Sun´va.

Sun´va and Eva both looked up from their work among the dead and injured to see who shouted so joyously in this place of death.

'Sun´va!' Cormac yelled again and ran wildly towards the girls, brandishing the head of Tullius on his sword.

'The head of Tullius the centurion!' he roared, looking from girl to girl. 'I bring you the head of Tullius the centurion.'

Sun´va and Eva both stepped back in alarm and disgust as Cormac thrust the gaping head, its black and swollen tongue lolling on its chin, under their noses.

'What!' cried Eva in horror. 'That poor man!'

'How did you get his head, you wicked, evil creature?' shouted Sun´va.

'Wicked!' Cormac threw back his head and gave a loud mock laugh. 'Evil! First you ask me for the head of the centurion, and then you tell me I am wicked to bring it to you!

What way is that to treat a warrior?' He still wasn't sure which one was Sun´va, so he addressed them both.

'That is my father's head,' protested Sun´va.

Shocked at her words, Cormac flicked the head off his sword and danced back from it as it rolled at his feet.

'How can it be your father's head?' he asked in a hoarse whisper, terrified at what he had done, and the punishment that would be sure to follow, and yet knowing she couldn't be right. 'I took this head myself, and it came off a Roman body, I'm sure of it. It is the head of Tullius the centurion.'

'Then it is my father's head,' Sun´va insisted. 'My father beat Tullius in single combat. Therefore the head is his by right. It is his battle-trophy.'

'Oh!' said Cormac as he realised what she meant. 'Well, your father can have his trophy for all I care. But that doesn't change our bargain.'

'Of course it changes our bargain,' said Sun´va.

This must be Sun´va, Cormac concluded, for she was the one he had made the bargain with.

'You don't think I am going to reward you,' Sun´va went on, 'for bringing me the head of a man that my own father killed!'

'The bargain said nothing about whose trophy it was,' Cormac said in a snarling voice. 'The bargain was that I was to bring you the head of Tullius the centurion, and there it is, look!' He gave the head a kick, as if it were no more than a turnip thrown into a field for the sheep. 'I brought it to you, and I claim ten thousand kisses from the daughter of Ultan! And remember, Sun´va, that if you do not keep your bargain, you will break your *geas* and your family will be cursed.'

But Sun´va was not listening. She was watching where

Ultan came slowly up the beach towards them.

'What is that head you have there, Sun´va?' Ultan called as he came near.

'It is your battle-trophy, father,' said Sun´va, scooping the head off the sands and holding it out towards her father. 'The head of Tullius the centurion.'

'But I did not take the head of the centurion,' said Ultan, taking the head now from his daughter and gazing into the red and swollen eyes. He pushed back the matted, sand-streaked hair from Tullius' forehead with a gesture that was almost tender.

'I took it, Ultan,' said Cormac proudly. 'I took it for you.'

Sun´va and Eva both gasped at this barefaced lie.

'And now I claim your daughter, Sun´va, to whom I am betrothed,' Cormac continued, pressing his luck.

Ultan gave Cormac no answer. This was no time for talk of marriage.

'Poor Tullius,' he said, half to himself, 'he fought well.'

He tucked Tullius' head under his arm and went with it in the direction of the shrine in the oakwoods, where the heads of defeated foes were kept. Cormac skulked away in the opposite direction, robbed of his trophy and defeated for the moment.

'I want to marry him,' Sun´va said, when she and Eva were alone.

'Cormac? Oh, I am so glad.' Eva clapped her hands. 'I know he drinks too much at times, but he is young and he is brave. He will make a fine man and you will influence him, Sun´va, to grow into a good one too. He's quite good-looking, have you noticed the way ...'

'Not Cormac!' Sun´va cut across her sister's delighted

chatter. 'I wouldn't marry him if he were the last man on earth. It is Fill-avius that I want to marry!'

'Sun´va! Be sensible, my dear sister, you can't possibly marry Flavius. He's the enemy.'

'But I love him,' said Sun´va. She threw her arms out to the sky and twirled, and as she twirled she chanted: 'I love his hair, I love his eyes, I love his arms. I love the very bones of him. I love his smile, I love his voice, I love the way …'

This time it was Eva who cut across her sister's raptures. 'I thought you said there was no such thing as love,' she said.

'I never said that,' said Sun´va, stopping suddenly. 'Did I?'

'Yes you did. Not six hours ago.'

'I was wrong,' said Sun´va with a shrug, and started twirling again. 'I know better now. I know better now. I know better now.'

'Stop!' said Eva. 'You're making me dizzy. What has happened to change your mind? How come you know better now?'

Sun´va stopped twirling and sat down abruptly on the damp sand.

'The battle,' she said with a shrug. 'Death. It's everywhere. But he is alive. It was only when I saw him coming forward to tend the body of Tullius, after my father had killed him, that I realised how desperately I had wanted him to survive. I could hardly believe that the gods had spared him. I knew then I wanted him above anything in the world. And I can have him; he's here, he's alive. It is flying in the face of fortune not to take this opportunity.'

'There is no opportunity,' argued Eva. 'He is still the enemy. He has to leave this place, with the other survivors, by sunset.'

'He could stay, couldn't he?' Sun´va said, in a pleading voice, as if it were up to Eva. 'When the others leave for Rome, they could leave him behind, couldn't they?'

'No, Sun´va, they couldn't,' said Eva. 'He doesn't speak our language. He doesn't belong here. And I'm sure he has a family at home. He can't just not go back to them. What about his mother? Or his wife?'

'He hasn't got a wife!' said Sun´va indignantly.

'How do you know?'

'He's too young.'

'He's not too young to be a soldier. He's not too young to marry you, according to yourself. What do you know about him? Nothing! You can't marry a stranger, Sun'va – someone you know nothing about. It doesn't make sense.'

'Sense, sense, who cares about sense?' said Sun´va impatiently. 'Or,' she added slyly, 'I could go with him. Elope.'

'Sun´va! You who love the very ground of Ireland. You going to Rome is just about as unlikely as him staying here. The problem is the same, except in reverse.'

'People can learn to live in other places. Slaves have to do it all the time.'

'Slaves! You want to live like a slave, Sun´va?'

'No, but …'

'That is exactly what you are describing, though, the life of a slave, far from home, among strange people, learning a strange language. Do you want to grow old like Gobnat?'

'No,' said Sun´va. 'No.'

The girls drifted apart then, and went back to their work, tending the wounded and washing the dead.

The Curiosity Tree 9

Cormac had wandered away, but he was not going to be cheated. He had made a bargain with Sun´va, and he had kept his side of the bargain in bringing her the head. It didn't matter who had actually killed the centurion: that was beside the point. He had to make her see that, and if she would not see it, he would make Ultan see it.

As the slaves gathered up the bowls and platters and jugs after the victory meal, he went and found Eva and told her that she would have to support him in his demand for the hand of Sun´va.

'You can see that I am merely holding her to the bargain we made, Eva, can't you?' he said. 'In fact, it was she herself who struck the bargain. I did not make her do it. She set the terms, and now she is trying to wriggle out of it. Well, she can't, and you are going to have to make her see that.'

'Why?' asked Eva tearfully. 'Why am I going to have to persuade her?'

'Because if you don't, she will break her *geas* and your whole family will be cursed.'

Eva knew the power of the *geas*. She was not sure if Cormac had the right to impose a *geas*, but she could see the logic of his argument, that Sun´va had herself been the one to set the terms of the bargain, and though she knew it was unjust, she could not see a way out of it for Sun´va.

'Suppose,' she tried feebly, 'suppose she offered to give you the ten thousand kisses here, now, on this beach, before you go home. That would be keeping her bargain. She doesn't actually have to marry you.'

'Hah!' said Cormac. 'Well, I do not propose to wait here long enough for her to kiss me ten thousand times. I leave tomorrow to go back to my own country. No, the only way that Sun´va can keep her word is to come with me, and the only way she can honourably do that is to marry me.'

Eva sighed and said she would try to speak to Sun´va.

'You'd better, Eva, daughter of Ultan,' said Cormac, 'or it will go ill with all of you.'

He drew his sword then and waved it at her.

'Daughter of Ultan,' whispered Eva to herself as Cormac waved the sword at her. 'I am the daughter of Ultan and I must save my family. I can do it. I can do it. I can.'

'I am going to find her!' yelled Cormac as he marched away from Eva, still brandishing his sword. 'I am going to force her if you won't persuade her. I know where she will be, where she always is when she is nowhere else to be found – it's well known around here where she hides herself.'

Hardly hearing him, Eva clapped her hands quickly as the thought came to her, and then at once she sat down hard on the ground and wept when she realised the full implications of her plan. But it was up to her. She was the one who had got them all into this sorry mess in the first place, by dancing with that handsome Roman boy, and it was up to her, Eva, to solve the problem. Eva was the only one who could save Sun´va from this dreaded marriage. She watched Cormac striding away with his sword still aloft, shouting Sun´va's name. I must follow him, she thought. I must tell him.

Cormac came to the curiosity tree and called Sun´va's name, but there was no reply. He climbed the tree himself, to be sure, but Sun´va was not among its branches. He settled himself into a fork where two of the highest boughs met the trunk, and looked out over the whole beach, waiting to catch sight of her.

Soon enough he saw her, racing towards the tree, and she had a Roman soldier by the hand. Cormac watched in outrage as she drew Flavius into the shadow of the tree.

Here at the entrance to the cool and shady, sweet-smelling woods, Sun´va and Flavius were well out of the infernal smoke and ash of death and the stench of cooking flesh on the beach. She'd found him, wandering disconsolately at the Irish end of the beach, still looking for Cormac, wanting to retrieve Tullius' head, so that he could restore it to the centurion's body and Tullius could present himself whole and entire at the gates of the Underworld.

'Here,' she whispered to him. 'We can lie down here. Come on. Come on.'

She pulled at Flavius as she sank onto the forest floor in the shade of the old tree, and he half slithered, half fell to her side and started to cover her face with kisses.

As their arms wound around one another, there came a deathly roar from the tree above them, and Cormac came hurtling down on top of them, flailing and screaming as he fell.

Sun´va was thrown to one side. She quickly scrambled to her knees and then to her feet. Cormac beat and slashed the air with his sword, guttural sounds coming from his throat like the grunts of some wild pig.

Flavius managed to get to his feet, but he had nothing, not even a stick, to use as a weapon, nor had he a piece of armour to save him from Cormac's onslaught.

'Fill-avius!' Sun´va screamed his name over and over, putting out her hands to try to save him from the blows of Cormac's sword.

'Stand back, Sun´va, keep away from him, he is mad!' Flavius cried, taking his eyes off Cormac for a moment in his anxiety for Sun´va.

Cormac saw his chance, when Flavius was distracted by Sun´va, and he lunged at him with a wild roar and made a swipe with his sword at the soft part of Flavius' body, where his ribcage divided.

Flavius staggered, not sure if he had really been stabbed with the sword. At the last moment, as he turned from Sun´va, he had seen the blade heading right for his middle, but he hadn't felt a cut or a stab, merely a blow as if someone had hit him in the stomach with a sack half-full of wet corn. He staggered back again, clutching his stomach.

He still could feel no pain, just this terrible sensation of being winded, which finally knocked him back off his feet. He hit his head on a tree root in the fall, and passed out. As he sank into oblivion he could hear Sun´va's screams and cries, but they were like the cries of birds far, far up in the sky. Poor bird, he thought as he went into the darkness. Poor bird.

Sun´va fell on his body, sobbing and crying and calling out his name over and over, 'Fill-avius, Fill-avius, Fill-avius!', but there came no reply. He did not so much as open his eyes or lift a hand to show her that he heard.

Dead, he must be dead. A fresh gust of tears and sobs

swept Sun´va's body. 'You've killed him,' she sobbed to Cormac, 'you've killed him, Cormac, you coward.'

'Give over, girl,' Cormac snarled. 'Give over. He is only a Roman. There is no need to make such a fuss. He is just one more dead Roman soldier. He might just as easily have been killed in battle.'

'You coward!' Sun´va yelled at him. 'You miserable coward! You went for an unarmed and defenceless man with a sword. You snivelling field mouse, you slithering reptile, you damnable water rat, you wretched creature.'

'Hold, hold!' called Cormac. 'That is no way to speak to your betrothed. I will not have my affianced wife call me names!'

'I will never be your wife,' sobbed Sun´va, 'never! You are not worthy of me, Cormac son of Cuan. I spit on you. I spit on you and I dismiss you and your retinue from this place.'

'It is not for you to dismiss me, Sun´va daughter of Ultan,' roared Cormac. 'For you are bound to me by the promise you made concerning the head of the centurion, and the *geas* I laid on you to observe your word.'

Sun´va did not even bother to argue. She just laid her head on Flavius' breast again and wept for him.

That is how Eva found them when she arrived some moments later: Flavius stretched on the ground, Sun´va distraught and Cormac still waving his arms about and laying claim to Sun´va.

'How can you want me?' Sun´va asked, raising her head. 'How can you possibly want a wife who hates and despises you?'

'I want you,' said Cormac, 'because you are mine. You promised yourself to me before the battle, you promised me ten thousand kisses if I brought you the head of the centurion, and I did, and now I claim you.'

Eva stepped forward. This was her moment.

'Cormac son of Cuan, your claim is accurate. It is not right, it is not fair, but in strict terms it is correct, because you were promised ten thousand kisses from the daughter of Ultan if you brought her the head of the centurion, and it is true that the bargain did not mention that the head should rightfully be yours to bring.'

Cormac gazed at her, breathing heavily.

'You see?' he said to Sun´va then, wiping the sweat from his heavy brow with the back of his forearm. 'Even your sister agrees.'

'But,' Eva went on, raising her palm to forestall Cormac, 'I too am the daughter of Ultan, and if you remember the bargain, there was nothing about which daughter of Ultan you should have. I offer you ten thousand kisses from the daughter of Ultan. Cormac son of Cuan, I will marry you to fulfil my sister's bargain and to protect the honour of my family.'

'Eva! No!' Sun´va raised herself from Flavius' body and went to her sister, grabbing her arms. 'Do not sell yourself into slavery in Meath. Do not give yourself to this unworthy man.'

'Sun´va,' said Eva, her voice steady, though she was shaking inside. 'It was because he thought I was you that Flavius danced with me, and it was this dance that led to the battle and to all this death and destruction, and so you see, it was because of me, and in particular because of me confused with you, that all this came about. And now I have a chance to redeem the situation and marry Cormac on your behalf, for I know that you cannot do it.'

'It wasn't because of you, Eva. And he's a wretch. He killed Flavius for nothing, just out of jealousy. You can't marry him.'

'He's not. He's stupid and weak and possessive. But he is not bad. When he has what he wants, he will calm down. When justice is done to him, he will see that we have been fair, and he will make a good husband for me, the second twin, who never thought to marry the son of a king.'

'Eva, no! Don't do it!'

'What do you say, Cormac?' Eva asked.

Cormac knew this was the best offer he was going to get, and after all, what was the difference? One sister looked exactly the same as the other, and this one would be less troublesome than Sun´va, that was certain.

'Very well,' he said, making it sound like a great concession. 'I will take you, Eva, in fulfilment of your sister's promise. You are the daughter of Ultan, and that was what was promised. It will do.'

Eva had not thought to marry a son of a king, but she did hope to marry a man who would be more gracious about her than this. However, she had made her decision, and she would stick by it. She held out her hand to Cormac and said: 'Cormac son of Cuan, I give you my hand. Let us go to my father and seek his blessing.'

Cormac threw a last glance at Sun´va and then he took Eva's proffered hand and the two of them went in search of Ultan.

As soon as they had left, Sun´va turned again to Flavius. There was very little blood. Perhaps the sword had not reached his heart. Very carefully, she drew open his shirt to examine the wound, and as she did so, Flavius opened his eyes and let out a long, slow moan of pain.

'Fill-avius!' she gasped. 'You are alive! Oh! Let me kiss you. Now, stay there, don't move, I am going for Gobnat. She has the power to heal. I am going for her now. Close your eyes, rest. I will be back.'

Flavius gave a crooked smile. '*Salve*,' he said.

She kissed him again and then she stood up and raced to the beach, her heart beating painfully in her chest.

CHAPTER 14

Who knocks so hard? Whence come you?
What's your will?
Romeo & Juliet Act 3, Sc iii

Jonathan phoned.

Lydia answered. Her head buzzed when she heard his voice. It seemed to reach that place she couldn't name, where she kept her sense of herself, hidden and fragile.

'Julia?' he asked, and Lydia's heart took a dive. It seemed to hang there, pumping away loudly, muscularly, in the space below her ribs.

'No,' she said grimly. 'It's the wrong twin.'

'You're not the wrong twin, Lydia,' said Jonathan, with surprising warmth. 'It's you I want to talk to. You just sounded like Julia, that's all. Anyway, she always answers the phone.'

'What do you want, Jonathan?' asked Lydia firmly. She wasn't going to let him get to her again, not after the last time. He was a weak-minded, hot-tempered boy who drank more than was good for him and made trouble wherever he went. And yet – she was weakening, she knew it – he'd always been nice to her, bought her coffee, made her laugh. She had no evidence for this boorishness that Julia kept accusing him of, apart from those cruel words to Tito on the night of the party

– but he hadn't been himself on that occasion. Also, he had the most wonderful eyes she'd ever looked into, which was a consideration.

'Well, I was just wondering …' he started.

'Where are you? It sounds very echoey.'

'Look, would you ever do me a favour, Lydia? Would you ring my mother and tell her that I've been … delayed. Tell her I won't be home for lunch.'

The pump in Lydia's gut worked harder.

'Why don't you ring her yourself?'

'I did. I can't get through, and I won't be able to ring again, so I thought I'd just ask you. I knew I could rely on you.'

Yes, thought Lydia ungraciously. That's Lydia. Reliable. But at least, for once, she was the right twin.

'Why won't you be able to ring again? What's going on, Jonathan? Are you on your mobile?'

'I lost it. Or broke it. Something. I … Lydia, I have to go. Will you ring my mother for me? I have no more coins.'

'Yes, of course I'll ring her, but she won't …'

'Thanks, Lyd. You're a star.'

The line went dead.

I'm a star, thought Lydia. And I'm the right twin. She put a hand over her stomach, to steady her heart.

As Lydia put the receiver down, the doorbell rang.

Lydia stared at the tall, broad guard who stood on the doorstep. He had a clipboard in his hand and he pointed with a large white freckled finger, the nail lined and ridged, to an African-looking name.

'Does Mrs Catherine Noowa– Nawee–, I'm sorry, I can't pronounce the surname. Does she live here?'

Lydia peered. 'Oh, that must be Catherine,' she said. 'No, she doesn't live here. She lives …'

Suddenly it crossed her mind that Catherine might not want to be found by the guards. She hesitated.

'You may as well tell me,' said the guard. 'I'll find out soon enough, and anyway, it's nothing bad. Or at least, it's nothing to do with her personally. I am looking for her on behalf of a young friend of hers. Tito Ac–, Ach–' Again, he pointed to an African surname.

'Oh, Tito! Yes,' said Lydia. 'But Tito knows where she lives. He lives there too.'

'I know that,' the guard said patiently. 'Tito told me that. But I thought he gave me this address.'

Lydia looked at the clipboard again.

'No, look, it's a bit smudged,' she said. 'It says twenty-three. Not twenty-five. This is twenty-five.'

'You're right, it's twenty-three,' said the guard, looking relieved. 'So that'd be next door, then. Which side?'

'What's going on?' Lydia asked.

'Oh, I couldn't tell you that,' said the guard grandly. 'That's confidential.'

'Is Tito in trouble?'

'I told you …'

'Look, he's a friend of ours. We'd want to help if there's a problem. They're not going to deport him, are they?' Lydia couldn't keep the panic out of her voice.

'Not at all,' said the guard. 'This is about something else.'

'Oh good!' said Lydia. 'Look, Catherine is out at w–' She stopped. She wasn't sure if Catherine was allowed to work, even voluntarily. '… at church,' she amended.

'At church?' asked the guard. 'On a Friday? Unless of course she's a Moslem.'

'Oh, she's very religious,' said Lydia quickly. 'She's always running off to … pray. Any day of the week. But the thing is, if Tito is in trouble, he would want us to help if Catherine isn't around, I'm sure of it. Really and truly he would.'

'Are you a Quinn?' the guard asked, flipping over a page on his clipboard.

'Yes!' said Lydia. 'Oh good, so he has mentioned us too.'

'Julia Quinn?' asked the guard.

'No,' said Lydia. 'I'm Lydia. Julia's my twin sister.'

'Ah,' said the guard. 'The Quinn Twins. Or, as you might say, the Twin Quinns.' His big shoulders heaved with laughter as he made his little joke.

'You might,' said Lydia coldly.

'Well, he's given Julia's name if Catherine can't be found. He didn't mention Olivia.'

'Lydia,' said Lydia.

'That's an unusual name,' said the guard. Then, seeing that Lydia was running out of patience, he added, 'But sure, I suppose, one twin is as good as another. Right, well, now, don't be alarmed, but he is above in the hospital, in casualty. He wanted to let this lady, Catherine, know where he is. I said I'd tell her, put her mind at rest. Is she his sister?'

'No,' said Lydia. 'Friend, neighbour. What happened? Was there an accident?'

'Not an accident,' said the guard. 'More a fight.'

'You mean, someone attacked him? Poor Tito!'

'I wouldn't say that exactly,' said the guard. 'It takes two to fight.'

'He doesn't fight,' said Lydia stoutly.

'You seem to know an awful lot about him,' the guard said.

Lydia blushed. 'Well, we're friends, we see a lot of each other. We're neighbours.'

'I'd say he's a good-looking young fellow all right,' said the guard astutely, 'when his face is its normal size.'

Lydia blushed harder.

'Is he very badly hurt?' asked Lydia.

'Well, no bones broken, I'd say,' said the guard, 'except maybe a few ribs. It's hard to tell with ribs. His face is a bit of a mess, but he'll be all right. His main problem is that he may well be charged with affray.'

'Affray?' said Lydia.

'Fighting.'

'But he wouldn't hurt a fly. It must have been a racist attack.'

'Well, to tell you the truth,' said the guard, 'that's what we thought ourselves, but Tito says no. He is absolutely adamant. He refuses to say anything to incriminate young Walker.'

'Walker! Is that Jonathan Walker?' Lydia's heart gave a lunge somewhere inside her, somewhere it wasn't supposed to be.

'I couldn't tell you that. It's confidential information. I didn't mean to mention even the surname.'

'Well, it has to have been Jonathan who attacked him. Wait till I …'

'Now, now,' said the guard. 'We don't know who attacked who.'

'Well, I know,' said Lydia grimly. 'Is Jonathan at the hospital too?'

'I shouldn't be telling you this,' said the guard, uncomfortably.

Lydia stared at him.

He relented. 'Yes, he is. And he's all right too, apart from a broken nose.'

'Good enough for him,' said Lydia. 'Well, anyway, thank you, Guard …'

'Mullen,' he said, and raised his cap a fraction off his forehead.

'Guard Mullen. I'll explain to Catherine, no problem. Is

there anything else we can do to help?'

'Not for the present,' said the guard.

'Well, look, would you give him my … give him our love, will you, please?'

'Your love?' said the guard. 'I suppose that'd be all right. I'll tell him. And I'll leave it up to you to talk to Mrs Na—, Catherine, so.'

'And tell Jonathan I'll murder him,' Lydia added, through gritted teeth.

'Now, now,' said the policeman again. 'Goodbye, Miss Quinn.'

Julia kept chewing on a corner of her duvet cover as Lydia told her the story. 'Poor Tito,' she said at intervals, 'oh, poor Tito.'

'You'll chew a hole in that thing,' said Lydia. 'Stop, can't you?'

Julia gave a final pull at the corner of the duvet cover with her teeth and then she dropped it, a small, damp triangle, on the bed. 'Will they deport him, do you think?' she asked Lydia.

'I don't know,' said Lydia, 'but I think it's unlikely you can be deported for getting in a fight, even if you started it, which we are sure he didn't. I don't think they actually do deport people much anyway, when it comes down to it.'

'I hope not, oh, I hope not!' said Julia. 'I blame that book.'

'What book?'

'*The Curiosity Tree*. It's about us, can't you see? That author has written our lives for us, only disguised. And now it's all coming true.'

'That's rubbish,' said Lydia. 'She never even met us. The book is about characters. She made them up. We're real. There's no connection.'

'Still, I can't help thinking … don't you think … doesn't it make you feel it's like a lesson or something?'

'No!' said Lydia. 'Books with lessons are horrible. It's a story, Jule, not a schoolbook. What lesson?'

Julia thought for a moment. 'About love, I suppose. About how you have to follow your love, because it's the most important thing, isn't it? That's what love stories are about really.'

'No,' said Lydia again. 'You haven't read it right to the end, have you? That's not what it's about at all. It's much more complicated than that.'

'Is it?' said Julia, picking the book off her bedside table and flipping to the last chapter.

'Look,' said Lydia. 'A story's a story and life is life. And one thing about life is, you can't live it in fear of unhappy endings. You have to live your life as it comes to you.'

'Do I?' said Julia.

'Yes,' said Lydia. 'That's the only way. Otherwise, we'd all go mad.'

The Curiosity Tree 🔟

Evening had descended as Sun´va went for Gobnat to come and tend Flavius, lying under the curiosity tree. The sun was almost gone: only a slender crescent of it was left above the horizon. As Sun´va hurried back again from the crannog, with Gobnat, the Roman boats were already on the water. They made dark shapes, stark against the backlit sky, and Sun´va could hear the oars splashing in the deep-blue sea. Good! They were going, and they were going without Flavius. She could keep him here, she could, she could. Gobnat would nurse him back to life and then Sun´va would marry him and it would all be wonderful!

Sun´va was not to know that while she was fetching Gobnat, Aurelius had been scouring the beach, the camp, the woods, looking for his comrade. And at last, at almost the last moment before the sunset deadline, he had found him, under an oak tree near the beach, semi-conscious, raving, claiming that Sun´va was going to come back to treat his wound. Aurelius could not leave his comrade there in the woods. He was tall and broad, twice Flavius' size. Hunkering down, he picked Flavius up and carried him in his arms. Flavius roared in protest, and in pain, but he had no strength to struggle, and Aurelius shushed him with comforting words as he staggered with him to the ships. And with the light rapidly fading, Aurelius had wedged Flavius, still screaming with pain but fully conscious now, between Marcus, who was babbling incoherently, and another of his comrades, where they crouched on deck. Then he went to join the line of unwounded men who would row the boats. The stars were just beginning to wink now in a sky that was barely navy.

'Fill-avius!'

Sun´va had reached the woods and found the beaten-down patch of grass still warm from Flavius' body, but no Flavius. She ran to the sea's edge.

Flavius looked up at the sound of the familiar voice and his heart leapt. Sun´va stood on the shore and waved to him. Her white figure was just visible on the darkening beach and her hair gleamed in the fading light. It was as if she had reached right out over the water to him and wrenched the heart out of his chest.

'*Veni!*' she called to him, using one of the words he had taught her on that first morning they had met.

It gave his heart such a painful squeeze when he heard that word from her lips that he had to gasp to breathe.

A guffaw went through the men in the boat.

'Made a conquest, there, eh, young Flavius? While the rest of us are making war, you're making love? And teaching her Latin to boot! Well, well, what it is to be young! And you hardly able to talk, much less walk!'

'Fill-avius!' came the call again.

Sun´va had climbed onto a rock at the shore now and was waving desperately to the boat. Surely he must see her, surely he could hear her. The drift of men's laughter came to her from the ship. They were only yards apart. He must hear her.

Flavius closed his eyes so he wouldn't have to see her pleading gestures. He could feel tears gather at the corners of his eyes, but what could he do? He was wounded and ill and he was on his way home to Rome, and anyway, he couldn't stay here with Sun´va, the daughter of a Celtic chieftain. It was an absurd idea, it would never work.

Cornelia loved him, he told himself. He would go straight to her as soon as he was well and they would be married, as planned.

'Fill-avius!'

The voice was getting fainter now, as the distance between them opened and stretched across the sea. The sound of the oars was a steady whir-splash, whir-splash, and with his eyes tightly closed, Flavius imagined every stroke taking him closer to Rome.

'Fill-a-a-vius,' Sun´va called, faintly, faintly, over the splashing water.

When Flavius dared to open his eyes again, Sun´va was like a wraith in the distance, a slip of almost nothing. What could he do? Maybe it still wasn't too late. He could tell the others he wanted to go back. He could ask them to row quickly to shore and let him off. Or, if they wouldn't agree to that, maybe he could get them to drop him overboard and let him take his chances in the sea. He had only a flesh wound. It wouldn't stop him swimming; it was nowhere near his arms. It was only a few minutes' swim to the shore. He could make it, no problem.

'*Veni!*' she called again. Or did she? Was it she who called or someone else?

He screwed up his eyes and strained to see, but the seeping black of nightfall had enshrouded her completely and now he could see nothing of her, nothing at all.

CHAPTER 15

It is my lady; O! it is my love!
Romeo & Juliet Act 2, Sc ii

The blaze of afternoon had long passed and the earliest mauve glimmerings of evening were stretching into the sky when Jonathan and Tito finally emerged from the Garda station. They shook hands, on the steps of the building, carefully because of their wounds.

They'd both been questioned and had been let off with a warning, which was due largely to the good offices of Guard Mullen.

'Good lads,' said Guard Mullen, in his fatherly way, holding both their elbows, one in each fist.

Then he caught the eyes of the twins, who had been waiting outside the station for the boys to be released, and he winked at them.

'Thank you, officer,' said Tito gravely, in his polite, foreign way.

'And now,' said the guard, turning to the boys. 'I think you lads should take these two fine lassies of yours off for a cup of coffee. And I never want to see any of ye within sight nor sound of this place again, all right?'

'Thank you,' Lydia said, and she stepped forward to shake his hand.

'Yeah, thanks,' the others muttered, half-embarrassed. Jonathan was kicking one foot with the toe of his other shoe. Julia was twisting a tissue into shreds. 'Thanks very much. Eh … yeah, thanks. You were … well, yeah, thanks anyway.'

Then Julia and Tito turned to each other and, without saying a word, twined their arms around each other's waists and walked ahead, like a single, three-legged creature, towards the darkening blue of the sea, Julia taking care to rest only lightly against Tito's battered and bandaged ribcage.

Lydia and Jonathan fell into step behind Tito and Julia.

'What happened?' Lydia asked Jonathan. 'We thought they'd never let you out. We thought you'd be charged for sure. How long were you in casualty? You must have been queuing for hours if …'

'God, my head hurts,' said Jonathan.

'Tell me about the fight,' said Lydia.

'I was drunk,' Jonathan said.

Tito twisted his head around. 'You were drunk,' he agreed, dryly, over his shoulder.

The four of them stopped, then, making a small knot on the street, to continue the conversation. Tito and Julia stood lightly enmeshed together. Lydia leant against a wall, with her knee bent and one foot flat behind her against the wall's base. Jonathan rested a hand further up Lydia's wall, and leaned into it, on his wrist.

'It was very late,' Jonathan said, 'almost morning, really. I couldn't find my house keys …'

He'd lost his house keys. He always carried them in his trouser pocket, and he couldn't understand how they'd gone missing. He could only have dropped them or left them somewhere if he had first taken them out of his pocket. He tried to remember if he had, but his muzzy head just got muzzier when he tried to think. He tripped, and steadied himself by reaching for a lamp-post. He looked down to see what he'd tripped over. The pavement sloped away dangerously from his view, and then came rushing back towards him. He made a Trojan effort to focus, but he could see nothing on the undulating concrete surface of the pavement.

Well, the keys were gone, there was no point in puzzling over how he'd lost them. The immediate problem was how he was going to get in home without waking his parents. His head got muzzier still as he tried to think out a plan. He leant his forehead against the lamp-post, grateful for its cool bulk, and tried to concentrate.

Then he saw something looming towards him in the half-dark street. A jacket and trousers, walking all by themselves, like a ghost, in the breaking dawn. He must be very drunk. He focused on the walking clothes and realised that Tito was inside them, that black fella Julia was so keen on. That's why he hadn't been able to see him at first in the dark, because he was black. He was sauntering invisibly along on the footpath, as if he owned the place, pretending to be a ghost, giving people frights in the night.

'I get nightmares,' Tito chipped in. 'I wake up in a sweat, heart pounding. I'm afraid to go back to sleep again, in case I fall back into the dream. So I get up and go for a walk in the night, clear my head.'

Jonathan had watched him coming closer. Tito had one hand in his pocket, and as Jonathan watched, he saw him draw it out, in a tight fist.

His keys! It came to him with the fractured logic of drunkenness. Of course. Tito'd got Jonathan's keys. He'd stolen them, out of spite, to make life difficult for Jonathan. The nerve, the bloody nerve! They come over here, they jump the housing queue, they take up all the jobs in shops and restaurants so the school students can't make any pocket money, they nab our girlfriends, and even a man's bloody house keys aren't safe!

'I was drunk,' Jonathan said again, by way of apology.

'That's no excuse,' said Lydia.

Jonathan had lurched forward, into Tito's path. Tito stopped.

'Jonathan?' he said.

That soft voice of his! Guilty as hell.

'Gimmemekeys!' muttered Jonathan.

'I beg your pardon?'

'Mekeys. Gimmemekeys.'

'Jonathan, I'm sorry, I don't understand what you are saying.'

Jonathan lurched forward again and pulled at Tito's wrist.

'Whatchagotthere? Openup. Openup.'

Puzzled, Tito held his hand out, to show Jonathan the love bean, sitting in the middle of his palm.

'Flaminchessnut!' said Jonathan, with a belch. 'Schoopid-effinchessnut! Wheresmekeys?'

'Keys?' said Tito, finally picking a word out of Jonathan's mutterings. 'I don't know about your keys.'

Jonathan lashed out wildly towards the keys that weren't, his flailing hand skimming the side of Tito's hand, which was still outstretched. The love bean tipped off Tito's palm and into the gutter.

Tito let a roar and knelt down to retrieve it, but it had rolled out of view.

'He went ballistic,' said Jonathan. 'Absobloodylutely ballistic! Didn't you, Tito?'

'I went completely crazy,' said Tito. 'He'd made me lose it, and Julia gave it to me! It was the *love* bean.'

'Oh!' Julia gasped softly again. She could see the anger crossing Tito's face once more as he spoke. She squeezed his fingers.

'It's OK,' said Tito to Julia. 'I found it later. It was stuck under a bunch of leaves, near the drain. It polished up fine again.'

'That's how it started,' said Jonathan. 'There he was, kneeling by the gutter, shouting and swearing in some foreign language I couldn't make head or tail of, and next thing he made a lunge for my ankles, brought me down with a smack on the pavement. After that, I don't remember much, but we beat the living daylights out of each other, didn't we, Tito?'

Jonathan touched his puffy face as he spoke, and Tito unconsciously mirrored his actions, fingering the bandage that covered his bruised cheek.

'Jealousy,' Lydia diagnosed. 'All that old jealousy over Julia.'

'No, no,' said Jonathan. 'I'm long over Julia.'

'Thanks a bunch,' said Julia. 'Glad I meant so much to you.'

'I mean, well, maybe you're right, Lydia,' Jonathan amended, with unusual meekness.

But Julia was not mollified. 'You are a danger to the public, Jonathan Walker,' she said. 'For goodness' sake, you can't be going around attacking people for nothing at all, just because you're drunk. It is pure good luck that one of you wasn't more badly hurt. And you could have got Tito into terrible trouble. You might even have got him deported. If it hadn't been for that nice guard …' Her voice was starting to get hysterical. She stopped for a moment, took a deep breath, and continued more quietly. 'You're going to have to learn to control yourself, Jono. Will you get a grip?'

'But I *didn't* attack him,' said Jonathan. 'It was *him* that went for *me*. I mean, I was sure he had the keys, and I did knock that old bean of his in the gutter, but that was an accident. When that happened, it was him attacked me, he pulled me down into that gutter and he laid into me.'

'Yes, well,' said Julia defensively, 'but you provoked him.'

'Look, I'm sorry, Julia, but me and Tito, we made it up ages ago, didn't we, Tito?'

'We are friends now,' said Tito gravely. 'Sometimes, a fight clears the air.'

'Rubbish,' said Julia, rounding on Tito now. 'Fighting makes things worse. You should know that, Tito.'

Tito didn't argue. He grinned weakly at Jonathan. Jonathan gave him the thumbs up and a wink. What would girls know about the way men did things? They were full of lovely theories about world peace and brotherly love. But you didn't get to be mates by thinking what a grand place the world would be if everyone was nice to each other, did you? Girls' notions were fine in theory, but when it came down to it, there was nothing like a good scrap to make you admire the other fellow's guts, which was every bit as important as seeing his point of view. Better, maybe.

Julia sighed a deep sigh. Lydia sighed too.

'God, I'm so hungover,' Jonathan muttered, fingering his temple. 'I can't believe I'm still hungover. I must have had an awful lot to drink.'

'Serves you right,' said Julia. 'But I'm glad you two are on speaking terms, I suppose.' Then, quite unexpectedly, she leant forward, out of Tito's grasp, and gave Jonathan a soft kiss on the bridge of his broken nose. 'Friends?' she said. 'Now that we have both recovered so admirably from each other, I mean.'

Jonathan touched an amazed forefinger to the place she'd kissed. Maybe the way girls did things wasn't so bad after all.

'Admirably?' he said with a grin. 'Yeah, admirably, I suppose you're right.'

'Anyway, Jonathan's got Maura now,' said Lydia stiffly.

'Maura?' said Jonathan. '*Maura?*'

'Isn't she your girlfriend?' said Lydia. 'Your *current* girlfriend, maybe I should say, considering the rate you seem to work at.'

'Girlfriend? Maura, my girlfriend! No way!'

Julia and Lydia looked disbelievingly at Jonathan.

'Well, you certainly looked friendly enough the other night,' said Lydia primly.

Julia backed her up. 'That's right,' she said, 'stitched together, you were.'

'Oh, she had a twisted ankle. She had to hang on to me for support, that's all. She's just a friend. Really. She's not the one I love.'

'So you're still in love with Serena, then, are you?' asked Julia. Serena was the Belly Dancer's real name.

'No,' said Jonathan. 'Serena was a mistake.'

'She was,' said Julia. 'That's true. A big mistake. Look, are we going for this coffee or not? Maybe they fed you two in that Garda station, but we missed our lunch over you, running around leaving messages with people, making phone calls. And our dinner, too, now I come to think of it. I'm starving. We brought you both some clean shirts, by the way.' She waved a plastic bag. 'We can't be seen with you looking like *that*.' And she pointed at the blood-streaked clothes the boys wore.

'Thank you,' said Tito.

'Yeah, thanks,' said Jonathan.

'You can put them on when we get to the coffee shop,' Julia went on practically. 'They have a toilet.'

'The coffee shop!' said Jonathan. 'I couldn't face food, but lead on anyway.' He made a forward-sweeping gesture. 'Maybe a nice glass of orange juice,' he added to himself.

Julia and Tito turned around, resettled their arms around each other, and walked on. Jonathan turned to Lydia and slipped his arm around her waist. She drew her breath in sharply. She felt her body go rigid with tension, inside the circle of Jonathan's arm. This wasn't how it was supposed to be.

'Well, Lydia?' he said softly. 'What about it? You and me?'

Lydia turned to look at him.

'You and me?' she asked, astonished. 'But …'

'I'll give up the booze,' he said, misunderstanding her

hesitancy. 'I'll have to anyway when training starts next term.'

'Gee thanks,' said Lydia, relaxing enough to give a small laugh.

'No, no,' he said, dropping his arm from around her, 'I mean, I'll give it up because it makes me nasty and you won't want a nasty boyfriend, will you? And anyway, I feel awful afterwards.'

'Boyfriend?'

'Lydia, how bluntly do I have to put this? I asked you out before, and you were so strange, so distant, I was afraid to ask to see you again. Then on the night of the party, you pushed me away, and sent me off into such a depression, I nearly beat up Tito that time too, only that your dad threw me out. And now, you seem not to understand English.'

'Oh, I do understand,' said Lydia, dithering. 'I wasn't distant, that time in the coffee shop, I was nervous, and I thought you only wanted to talk about Julia …'

'Julia? I only mentioned her because I couldn't think of what to say to you. She was what we had in common. That's all.'

'And at the party,' Lydia went on, 'I thought … I thought you were with Maura, I mean you *were* with Maura, but I mean *with* her, I mean, I just don't …'

'Do you know what it is?' said Jonathan. 'If my nose didn't hurt so much, I'd kiss you, even if it was only for the sake of shutting you up.'

'Oh!' said Lydia. 'Sorry.'

'I'm joking, Lydia,' Jonathan said. 'About shutting you up, I mean, not about … Would you look at those two!'

He jerked his thumb in the direction of Julia and Tito. They had stopped in the doorway of the cappuccino bar, and were locked in a passionate kiss, blocking the way in and out and blissfully unaware of it.

'It gets you going,' said Jonathan, 'doesn't it?'

'Oh!' Lydia gasped, watching.

Julia was leaning carefully against Tito, not wanting to squeeze his sore ribs, and he held her gingerly. They should have looked awkward, uncomfortable, all wrong. But they didn't. They looked perfect together, absolutely perfect.

Lydia turned to Jonathan, seeing him as he really was – bluff, loud-mouthed, easily led. But then again, just being close to him did the most extraordinary things to her. And what was the point in anticipating trouble? She'd done that all her life, and how far had it got her? Her own advice to Julia rang in her ears. You can't live in fear of unhappy endings. You must live life as it comes to you. There's no other way.

Jonathan raised his eyebrows and opened his arms. Her heart started its crazy pumping again. Eva flickered through her mind. Well, I'm not *marrying* him, she thought. It's not irretrievable. Maybe she should give him a chance, give it a whirl, as Julia would put it.

'I tell you what,' she said, 'I'll mind your nose.'

She snaked her arms around his neck. A whirl, yes, a whirl, she was all of a whirl.

He couldn't believe his luck. 'Right,' he said, and drew her close, turning the best side of his face towards her.

The evening star wavered over the deepening bay, in a sky that ran to translucent turquoise, but none of the four noticed its steady progress from pale to bright as light seeped slowly from the surrounding sky, nor did they care.

ALSO BY SIOBHÁN PARKINSON

SISTERS ... NO WAY!

Cindy, still traumatised by her mother's recent death, is appalled when her father starts dating one of her teachers, who has two daughters of her own, Ashling and Alva. There could not be a worse fate than having a *teacher* as a stepmother, and as for those two prissy girls – she is never going to call them sisters ... no way! But if Cindy dislikes her prospective stepsisters, they think she is an absolute horror – spoiled, arrogant and rude They can't imagine being landed with Cindy as a sister ... no way! A flipper book tells the story from both sides: Cindy's and Ashling's.

Paperback €6.34/STG£4.99/$7.95

FOUR KIDS, THREE CATS, TWO COWS, ONE WITCH (maybe)

Beverly, a bit of a snob, cooks up a plot to visit the island off the coast. She manages to convince the somewhat cautious Elizabeth and her slob of a brother, Gerard, to go with her. A surprise companion is Kevin, the cool guy who works in the local shop. This motley crew get more than they bargained for when they become stranded on the island and encounter a very strange inhabitant.

Paperback €6.95/STG£4.99/$7.95

AMELIA

The year is 1914 and Amelia Pim will soon be thirteen. There are rumours of war and rebellion, and Dublin is holding its breath for major, dramatic events. But all that matters to Amelia is what she will wear to her birthday party and how she will be the envy of her friends. But where are Amelia's friends when disaster strikes her family? Now that the Pims have come down in the world, what use will Amelia have for a shimmering emerald-green dress? When Mama's political activities bring the final disgrace, it is Amelia who must hold the family together. Only the friendship of the servant girl Mary Ann seems to promise any hope.

Paperback €6.34/stg£4.99/$7.95

NO PEACE FOR AMELIA

It's 1916 but Amelia Pim's thoughts are on Frederick Goodbody and not on the war in Europe. Then Frederick enlists. The pacifist Quaker community is shocked, but Amelia is secretly proud of her hero and goes to the quayside to wave him farewell. For her friend Mary-Ann there are problems too, due to her brother's involvement in the Easter Rising. What will become of the two young men? And what effect will it have on the lives of Amelia and Mary Ann?

A story of conflict, hope and courage. Sequel to the No.1 bestseller Amelia.

Paperback €6.34/stg£4.99/$7.95

CALL OF THE WHALES

Over three summers, Tyke journeys with his anthropologist father to the remote and icy wilderness of the Arctic. Each summer brings short, intense friendships with the Eskimos, and adventures 'which Mum doesn't need to know about'. Tyke is saved from drowning and hypothermia, joins a bowhead whale hunt, rescues his new-found Eskimo friend, Henry, from being swept away on an ice floe, and witnesses the death of innocence with the killing of the narwhal or sea unicorn. A story that will echo in the mind long after the Northern Lights have faded from the final chapters.

Paperback €6.95/stg£4.99/$7.95

THE MOON KING

Ricky has withdrawn from the world into his own inner space. Placed in a foster home that is full of sunshine and goodness, he is uncertain how to become part of family life. He often retreats to his favourite hideaway, a special chair in the attic, and adopts the pose of the Moon King. From this situation relationships slowly begin to grow, but it is not a smooth path and at times Ricky just wants to leave it all behind. Can he learn to trust people again?

Paperback €6.34/stg£4.99/$7.95

AND FOR OLDER READERS

BREAKING THE WISHBONE

A group of teenagers, adrift from their families, scrape together a makeshift home in the House that Everyone Forgot. According to Johnner, it's like camping, like being on your holidays all the time. But then, Johnner's just a kid. They find out soon enough, all of them, just how harsh life is when you're young, poor and homeless. The reality of living rough in a Dublin squat poses more difficult challenges in their already troubled lives.

Paperback €6.34/STG£4.99/$7.95

Send for our full-colour catalogue